"*You aren't responsible for what happens to me, Garrett.*"

"You became my responsibility the moment I brought you home," he refuted gruffly.

Jenna was touched by his chivalrous sentiment, and startled by the deeper layer of resentment she detected in his tone.

"Why did you do it?" she asked quietly. "You could have left me to fend for myself."

He scoffed at that. "Sweetheart, you were far from being able to take care of yourself. You were in no shape to be left alone, and your options were limited. I was your safest bet."

"Thank you."

He shrugged off her gratitude. "So, what do you plan on doing now?"

"You mean now that I'm no longer someone's bride?"

NEARLYWEDS

Almost at the altar—
will these *nearlyweds* become *newlyweds*?

Welcome to Nearlyweds, our brand-new miniseries
featuring the ultimate romantic occasion—weddings!
Yet these are no ordinary weddings: our beautiful brides
and gorgeous grooms only *nearly* make it to the altar—
before fate intervenes and the wedding's...*off!*

But the story doesn't end there....
Find out what happens in these tantalizingly emotional
novels by some of your best-loved Harlequin Romance®
authors over the coming months.

Look out in July for
To Catch a Bride
by Renee Roszel
#3660

THE WEDDING SECRET

Janelle Denison

NEARLYWEDS

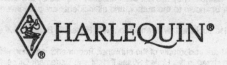

HARLEQUIN®

TORONTO • NEW YORK • LONDON
AMSTERDAM • PARIS • SYDNEY • HAMBURG
STOCKHOLM • ATHENS • TOKYO • MILAN • MADRID
PRAGUE • WARSAW • BUDAPEST • AUCKLAND

To my niece, Brianna—
may you find a hero as strong and handsome as your dad.
As always, to Don,
for being all that, and more.

ISBN 0-373-03653-1

THE WEDDING SECRET

First North American Publication 2001.

Copyright © 2001 by Janelle R. Denison.

This edition published by arrangement with Harlequin Books S.A.

Visit us at www.eHarlequin.com

Printed in U.S.A.

CHAPTER ONE

THE bride had the face of an angel and the body of a goddess, all wrapped up in yards of shimmery white fabric that spilled like liquid satin all around her. The incongruity of so much lily white material in an establishment where sinful fun was a Saturday night invitation made Garrett Blackwell do a double take as he slid onto a vacant stool at the bar.

He wasn't the only one staring at the lone bride occupying the far corner booth, drinking, or rather gulping, dark liquid from a snifter. Leisure Pointe was rocking with loud music and rowdy as ever with good-natured arguments and boisterous laughter, but the main attraction seemed to be the lady in white. The women eyed her with curiosity and speculation, while any one of the men looked willing and eager to stand in for the nonexistent groom.

Garrett couldn't blame them. She was a head-turner, the kind of woman a man could make a real fool of himself over. Huge blue eyes, full lips that begged to be kissed, and flawless, satiny skin that seemed to glow with warmth. Hair the color of sun-dappled wheat was pinned on top of her head, half of which had escaped to fall in a riot of springy, spiral curls around her face and down her back. The off-the-shoulder design of her wedding gown, dazzling with pearls and sequins, dipped low enough to hint at nicely rounded breasts, then nipped in to what appeared to be a tiny waist. He imagined she

5

had long, slender legs to match, and cut off his thoughts before they traveled to more forbidden territory. What skimpy lingerie she might be wearing beneath that dress was none of his business.

"She's a looker, isn't she?"

Garrett finally turned on his stool and faced Harlan, the burly man who tended the bar and owned the joint. Harlan wore a plaid flannel shirt with the sleeves rolled to just below his elbows, old worn jeans, and suspenders to hold them up, though the thick girth of his belly could have done the job just as easily.

"What she looks like is someone who made a wrong turn off of Interstate 44 coming out of St. Louis." No one as city-polished and elegant as her would deliberately head to the small town of Danby, Missouri, unless they'd gotten lost. "Who is she, anyway?"

"Damned if I know." Harlan pried open a long-neck and set the bottle in front of Garrett, knowing his preferred drink. "Nobody seems to know who she is or where she came from. Never seen her around Danby before tonight, and she's got a face and a body no healthy, red-blooded man would forget, if you know what I mean."

Oh, Garret knew exactly what Harlan meant. He didn't have to turn around to remember what she looked like, to recall the wild crush of hair a man could lose his hands in, full breasts made more lush by her slim waist, or to experience that unwanted stirring of desire that had skirted the edges of his own sanity. Shifting in his seat, he lifted the bottle of beer to his lips and took a long drink of the cool, malty liquid in an attempt to banish his wayward thoughts. "So, where's the groom?"

Harlan cleared dirty glasses off the counter and set them in the soapy water filling the sink behind the bar. "Haven't seen one, though she's had a few marriage proposals from the young bucks here tonight. They've been swarming around her like flies on a horse's tail, and making a general nuisance of themselves." He shook his head, something fiercely protective lighting his brown eyes, the kind of look one would expect from the father of three teenage daughters nearing the dating age. "I finally had to tell them to back off and leave her alone. She doesn't look like she's interested in the kind of company they have in mind, though that hasn't stopped some of them from sending her drinks. Five snifters of Amaretto. I just told Becky to cut her off and not to accept any more orders from her admirers, unless it's for coffee."

A smile twitched the corner of Garrett's mouth. Harlan appeared and acted like a big, gruff grizzly, but he was a kind and fair man. He ran his establishment efficiently and didn't begrudge a person a good time. But it was also known by anyone who frequented the place that Harlan didn't like trouble in his bar, didn't allow arguments to escalate into brawls, and he always looked after the patrons who'd imbibed beyond their limit.

Like the bride without a groom.

Harlan moved to the opposite end of the bar to fill drink orders, and Garrett found his gaze sliding her way again. She was a fascinating feminine creature, made more intriguing by the mysterious circumstances that had brought her to Danby, and how out of place her presence was in Leisure Pointe. Dressed like a fairy princess, and possessing a natural beauty that was as stunning as it was arousing, she was like a glittering diamond nestled among drab rhinestones. She didn't belong, and had city sophistication written all over her.

When Harlan returned, Garrett expressed his thoughts out loud. "Who in their right mind would drop her off here?"

"Her limousine driver."

Garrett frowned. "I didn't see a limo out front."

Grabbing the bar towel slung over his shoulder, Harlan dried a beer glass and set it in the rack above him. His mouth stretched into a tight line of disgust. "The guy didn't stick around. He followed her in with a suitcase and told me that she asked him to stop here. The prissy fellow said his contracted time was up, that he wasn't waiting around, and she was on her own."

"That's it?"

"He did mutter something about having to drive all the way back to St. Louis, so I'm assuming that's where she came from."

But it explained little else.

Harlan sighed and braced a beefy forearm on the bar surface. "I need you to do me a favor, Blackwell."

Garrett lifted a brow. "Why do I get the feeling I'm not going to like what you have to say?"

"Aw, come on," Harlan groused. "I just want you to go over there and ask the lady who we can call to pick her up."

The request was simple, straightforward, and required minimal interaction, but Garrett didn't do damsels in distress—not anymore. Not when the last woman he'd rescued had taken advantage of his generosity and duped him in a very life-altering way.

His expression must have conveyed his grim thoughts because Harlan was quick with a response. "I'm sure I could get a line of volunteers to do the deed if I asked, but I suspect that most of the men in here would proposition her instead. Considering the frame of mind she's in…"

Garrett scowled. Harlan's words didn't paint a pretty picture. Dammit all, anyway, he thought irritably. He'd come to Leisure Pointe to relax and unwind, have a few beers and shoot the breeze with Harlan and some of the old cronies who'd been his dad's buddies before he'd died. The same old boring Saturday evening routine—so unlike his brother's weekend of partying, women, and generally raising hell with his own friends.

Rylan. Seeing a way out of Harlan's well-meaning intentions, Garrett squinted through the haze of cigarette smoke in the bar, searching for a dark, tousled head of hair and a quick charming grin that belonged to his younger brother.

"Why don't you find Rylan and get him to do it?" Garrett suggested. Though his brother enjoyed the fairer sex, and they flocked around him like bees to honey, he'd never take advantage of a woman. The honor and respect their mother had instilled in her boys was deeply ingrained, but Garrett doubted Charlotte Blackwell would ever have anticipated the steep price her eldest son had paid for being so chivalrous.

His eight-year-old daughter was a constant re-

minder of just how honorable he'd been. Too bad
Chelsea's mom hadn't been equally responsible, or
faithful—to him, or the little girl she'd never truly
cared about.

"Your brother left with Emma Gentry over an
hour ago," Harlan said. "And he didn't look like
he was going to be back any time soon."

Garrett wasn't surprised. He and his brother
shared the same house, which Garrett had inherited
from his mother when she'd moved to Iowa to live
with her sister four years ago. But at twenty-six, Ry
came and went as he pleased. More often than not,
Friday and Saturday nights were spent elsewhere.
Garrett didn't care with whom, as long as Ry stayed
out of trouble.

"How about Otis?" Garrett eyed the man sitting
at the far end of the bar. "He's pretty harmless and
can do the job just as well as I can."

"Otis is a randy old fart." Harlan glanced at the
other man, then back at Garrett, a dark frown bunching his bushy brows. "Just look at him. He's gawk-
ing at her, his mouth is hanging open, and he's all
but drooling! Do you honestly think he'd be able to
put together a coherent sentence when he's so obviously tongue-tied?"

Garrett couldn't help but laugh, and as his gaze
scanned the males sitting at nearby tables, he realized that Otis wasn't the only one lusting over the
voluptuous bride. Amazing that one woman could
have such an effect on so many men.

"For crying out loud, Blackwell, I'm not asking
you to marry the girl." Harlan was back to arguing,
and his brand of good-natured harassment, all the
while mixing drink orders on the pad in front of him.

"It's getting late, and if she lives in St. Louis, it's going to take someone a good hour to come and get her."

"Fine," Garrett said, feeling duly chastised for resisting such a quick and simple task for a friend. "You owe me, Harlan."

"Yeah, yeah." A sudden twinkle entered Harlan's eyes, one that matched the slow, satisfied grin on his face. "Go on. I'll have a cold one waiting for you when you get back."

Garrett grumbled one last complaint that did nothing to change Harlan's mind. Sliding off his bar stool, he headed toward the corner booth. The sooner he got this awkward errand over with, the sooner he could resume his mundane Saturday night activities.

Many curious eyes watched Garrett's progress across the room, making him uncomfortably aware of how conversations stalled as he passed by tables. This was a first...Garrett Blackwell approaching a woman in Leisure Pointe. It was a known fact that he didn't consort with the females in Danby beyond a polite nod or greeting. The few bolder, wilder ones that had attempted to pursue him he'd turned down as tactfully as possible, no matter how enticing the offer.

He'd never been one for gratuitous sex, but he wasn't a monk, either. Far from it. The few women whom he'd had affairs with over the years lived in other towns where gossip and speculation couldn't touch them, or his family. The women he chose to date also knew and accepted up front that he wasn't looking for anything serious. He had no intention of letting any woman manipulate his emotions again.

Blowing out a deep breath, Garrett severed those thoughts and opted to slide into the booth opposite where the bride sat, instead of standing at the edge of the table to conduct his business. The cozy corner table afforded him and the woman a modicum of privacy, away from most prying eyes and ears. The last thing he wanted to do was embarrass her, or provide entertainment for the masses.

She'd been staring into the depths of the dark liquid swirling in her snifter, looking so lost and dejected. Confused even. As soon as his jeans-clad legs tangled with the froth of satin beneath the table she glanced up, startled by his sudden appearance.

He opened his mouth to speak, and found himself broad-sided by the color of her eyes. At a distance, he'd been able to detect that they were blue, but up close and personal, they were incredibly striking—a soft shade of periwinkle, rimmed in a darker sapphire with the tiniest threads of gold shot through the middle. Her lashes were long and thick, her brows delicately, perfectly arched. A natural beauty mark just above her lip on the left side drew his gaze to her full, soft mouth. A mouth that inspired a dozen provocative thoughts.

Despite the symbol of purity and innocence her wedding gown implied, there was a natural, subtle air of sensuality about her. A contradiction of guilelessness and allure that aroused a man's basic interest. Yet he got the distinct impression that she wasn't aware of her appeal, didn't know the mesmerizing effect she had on men. She didn't flaunt herself, didn't tease or flirt to attract attention. She didn't need to. Mother Nature had blessed her—or cursed her, depending on how she viewed the situation—with a perfect face and body and a vibrancy that seemed to naturally radiate outward.

And then she wet her bottom lip with her tongue. Nothing sly or calculated about the gesture, but it certainly grabbed his attention and caused an unmistakable heat to thrum through his veins.

He suddenly felt ridiculously tongue-tied.

A sweet smile lifted her enticing mouth, but it didn't erase the haunting shadows in her eyes. Blinking slumberously, she slouched onto the table and propped her chin in her palm. She stared up at him in a dreamy sort of way, an effect he attributed to the alcohol she'd consumed.

"Hi." The one word floated to Garrett on a husky sigh of breath, wrapping around his already overloaded senses like a silky, physical caress.

Clearing his throat, he forced himself to remember his manners. "Ma'am. Are you okay?"

"I'mmm...fine," she said brightly, and gulped the last little bit of liquor in her snifter. "I'm jus'...great."

She was far from fine, and closer to the despair fringing her false bravado. "How about I buy you a cup of coffee?"

Her brows creased as she thought about his question. "Yeah, I think I could use some coffee. Lots of cream and sugar." She yawned, and her lashes drooped. "No more Armar...etto. It's making me sooo seepy." She giggled at her slur, then tried, "I mean ti-erd."

Stifling a grin, he motioned for the bar waitress and ordered the woman a cup of strong, black coffee. When he glanced back at the bride, he found her brushing at an unmanageable curl along her cheek, which kept springing back into place. A look of utter disgust flitted across her face.

"I hate my curly hair," she grumbled, blowing a frustrated stream of breath at the unruly strand. "Stupid curls never stay where I put them. Did you know I wanted straight hair when I was a little girl?"

"Uh, no." How could he have possibly known something so personal when he'd never met her before this evening?

Her eyes drifted closed, and just when Garrett thought she'd fallen asleep she spoke in a soft, wistful voice. "Every birthday I'd blow out the candles on my cake and wish for straight hair like my friend Cindy. It never happened."

He took in the long, lustrous hair she seemed to curse, too fascinated by those springy, natural curls and the way they might cling to his fingers...or how the caress of the sun might turn the strands to rich gold.

Her eyes fluttered open a moment later, a wealth of vulnerability shining in their depths. Unsure how to reply to her strange conversation, and feeling way out of his element, he played it safe and remained quiet.

"My other wishes didn't come true, either," she confessed quietly. "I was supposed to marry a prince charming, and live happily ever after. I guess I'm just not very good at making wishes."

Becky arrived with the coffee, saving him from having to formulate some kind of response. He knew the liquor was partially responsible for loosening her tongue, but he sensed her babbling about prince charmings and wishes somehow tied into the reason why she'd skipped out on her wedding day.

"Today was suppos' to be the happiest day of my life," she said once they were alone again, her soft voice quivering with emotion. "That's what my mom told me before she died, but it's the worst day of my life. All I wanted was a teensy-weensy bit of re-spec-ta-bil-ity, but I'll never, ever be respectable."

Aw, hell. What offense had she committed that was so awful she believed herself unworthy of respect? Compassion stirred within him, along with a good dose of curiosity over her comment. He quickly stifled both, refusing to tangle himself in this woman's emotional turmoil. Once he gleaned some pertinent information from her so Harlan could contact someone to pick her up, his duty would be done and he could get back to that cold beer Harlan had promised him.

And forget about this complex, periwinkle-eyed angel who seemed so lost and alone, and very vulnerable...and a possible scandal waiting to happen. The last thing he wanted or needed was speculation into his private life, and this mysterious woman would definitely provide that.

Scrubbing a hand over his jaw, he reached for the cream and sugar and poured a generous amount of each into her coffee, as she'd requested, and pushed the mug in front of her, urging her to drink.

She took a great shuddering breath, and lifted her troubled gaze to his. "Do you think when I wake up tomorrow this will all be just a bad, horrible dream?"

He wished he could offer her that assurance, but

instead tried to console her with an easy smile. "If you don't drink some of this coffee, tomorrow you're gonna end up with a bad, horrible hangover."

A frown marred her delicate brows and she picked up the mug, wrapping both hands around the warm ceramic. "I'm fine. Jus' great."

"Uh-huh," he agreed, humoring her, knowing if she tried to stand at the moment she'd fall flat on her pretty face. Resting his fingers beneath the bottom of her mug, he guided it toward her mouth. Her lips settled over the rim, and she took a drink and cringed, at the sweetness or the strength of the coffee, he couldn't be sure.

"What's your name?" he asked, figuring he'd start with simple questions and work his way up to the more difficult ones as her mind cleared.

"Jenna Chestfield..." Confusion etched her expression as she considered that name, then she shook her head, causing more of those unruly strands to spill from the top of her head and curl on the soft swells of her breasts straining the bodice of her gown. "No, we never said 'I do', so I guess I'm still just Jenna Phillips."

Just Jenna Phillips. There was a story in that, Garrett was sure, one he didn't want to get involved in, he reminded himself as his gaze drifted to her left hand. The absence of a ring on her finger backed her claim that no marriage had taken place.

She propped her chin in her palm again, as if her pretty head was getting too heavy for her shoulders to support. Her eyes grew soft, slumberous. "What's your name?"

"Garrett," he replied, deciding to keep things between them on a first-name basis.

"Garrett," she repeated, her husky voice making his name sound very intimate coming from her lips. "That's a nice, strong, respectable name. Are you respectable?"

Abrupt laughter rose in his throat, but he had the good manners to catch it before it escaped. Wanting to get his *chivalrous* deed over with, he asked, "Jenna, is there someone we can call to come pick you up?"

She didn't have to think long. "No."

He found that hard to believe. "Any family?" Remembering that she'd mentioned that her mother was deceased, he prompted, "Your father, or other relatives?"

She blinked, and an inexplicable sadness filled her eyes, a deep-rooted loneliness that struck a chord in him. "Nope," she whispered in an aching voice. "No one."

"How about your fiancé?" he asked. "Can we call him?"

She flinched at the mention of the man who would have become her husband, and her distress returned. He caught a wealth of regret, remorse and insecurities in her eyes before she cast her gaze downward.

"No, he wouldn't want me anymore," she said in a voice choked with certainty. "Not after the way I humiliated him and his family. I can't ever go back."

Another frustrating surge of sympathy gripped Garrett, and he valiantly tried to ignore it. He didn't want to care about this woman and her predicament, or why she believed she was such a big disappointment to the man she'd been engaged to marry.

Great. Now what should he do? He glanced over

at the bar and met Harlan's questioning gaze. Other than the woman's name, and learning that Jenna Phillips was seemingly as much of a loner as himself, he didn't have much more information on her than he had when he'd first sat down.

Well, he'd done his duty. Now, it was up to Harlan to figure out what to do with the lone bride for the night. He started to ease back out of the booth, but she grabbed his arm, which immediately stopped him. Her hand was soft and very cool against his heated skin, throwing images into his mind of how supple the rest of her body might feel beneath his calloused fingers, against his lips. He inwardly cursed—had he been that long without a woman that a stranger, and someone else's bride at that, could make him burn with a mere touch?

She'd latched on to him for security, that much was obvious. Meeting her suddenly desperate gaze, he banished those former thoughts from his mind, reminded himself he was done rescuing women, and tipped his head in inquiry.

"Are you leaving me?" Panic tinged her voice, as if she'd just realized that she was in a strange, distant town, in a rowdy, honky-tonk bar filled with men eager to take the place he was about to vacate.

"I just need to go talk to Harlan. Nobody will bother you," he promised, feeling uncharacteristically protective toward this woman he didn't know. Not a good sign. He wanted to say it was the same kind of paternal feeling he experienced with his daughter, but there was nothing nurturing about the awareness Jenna evoked. No, his response to her was all male and too threatening to the secure, stable life he'd built for himself and Chelsea the past six years.

And the sooner she found her way back to St. Louis and the life still waiting for her—a life certainly more sophisticated and exciting than this small, mundane town of Danby—the better off they'd all be.

He nodded toward her mug. "You finish up that coffee, all right?"

Her fingers tightened on his arm. "You'll come back?"

He wanted to say no, but the beseeching way his damsel in distress looked at him got under his skin, made him feel things he hadn't felt in too many years. "Yeah, I'll come back."

If only to help her out to a cab, or to make sure she was safe somewhere for the night, he told himself. That would be the extent of his involvement with this lost, complex bride.

"Are you out of your ever-lovin' mind?" Garrett gaped at Harlan as he absorbed the bartender's absurd suggestion. "I can't take her home with me!"

"Come on, Garrett," Harlan said, giving him a what's-the-big-deal kind of look. "I'm sure she'll be in a better frame of mind in the morning, and she'll realize her mistake and go back to wherever she came from. *One* night, Blackwell, not a lifetime."

One night was one night too many in Garrett's mind—not when this runaway bride affected his libido and emotions so strongly. "Find someone else to be your scapegoat, Harlan."

The bartender's gaze swept the rowdy room of

patrons, and returned to Garrett on a serious note. "I don't trust anyone else."

A vein in Garrett's temple throbbed with frustration, and he rubbed the offending spot with his fingers. "I don't do strays," he bit out in a last-ditch effort to convince Harlan that he was the wrong man to take care of Jenna Phillips. The only women he ever wanted to feel any obligation toward were his daughter, his mother, and his sister, Lisa.

Harlan swiped his towel over the gleaming mahogany surface of the bar, and sighed in resignation. "Then I guess I'll just have to call the sheriff to come and pick her up, and she'll have to spend the night down at the station in a holding cell."

Harlan moved away to fill a drink order, leaving Garrett with a restless unease tightening his belly. He glanced toward Jenna, who looked so bewildered and lost, and imagined this beautiful, soft-skinned, city-bred bride waking up in the morning on a narrow cot, disoriented and fearful, and without a shred of that respectability and dignity she'd wished for earlier.

Indecision warred within Garrett, and he struggled with those more gallant tendencies his mother had instilled in him. He didn't need the responsibility of taking care of this confused female, he argued with his conscience. He didn't need the complication of embroiling himself in her problems, he thought irritably. And he sure didn't need the distraction of her sleeping in his house, even for a night.

During Garrett's silent brooding, Beau Harding, a drifter who worked at the lumber mill in town, sidled up to the bar. Garrett nodded toward the other man in polite acknowledgment, but there was something about Harding Garrett didn't like, or trust. The young man was too arrogant for his own good. A month ago he'd come by Garrett's company, Blackwell Engineering, looking for work for the summer. Though Garrett had been considering adding on an extra man to his crew, he'd gone with his gut instinct and turned him away.

Beau cast a leer over his shoulder toward Jenna, then grinned wolfishly at Harlan as the bartender returned to their end of the bar. "Hey, Harlan, what's up with that lovely bride over in the corner?"

"We're just trying to figure out what to do with her," Harlan replied, very reluctantly.

Beau's pale gray eyes glimmered with interest. "You need someone to take her to a motel for the night?"

The innuendo in Beau's voice was unmistakable. The mere thought of this man touching Jenna, or possibly taking advantage of her current state, made Garrett feel unexpectedly territorial.

"No," he snapped before Harlan could respond. "She already has a place to stay."

Harlan's brows rose in surprise, considering how adamantly Garrett had refused any involvement with the bride only moments ago.

Beau's insolent gaze slid to Garrett. "Just thought I'd offer my assistance," he drawled, then sauntered away.

Garrett just bet Beau would like to *assist* Jenna. His temper flared like wildfire in his blood, startling him with the level of possessiveness she inspired. The last time he'd experienced such an overwhelming reaction had been over another woman. Chelsea's mother, to be exact.

And that encounter had led to nothing but grief, heartache, and a lingering bitterness over being used and betrayed.

"I'll go get her suitcase from the storeroom," Harlan offered, then quickly disappeared to retrieve Jenna's luggage, as if he feared Garrett might change his mind if he didn't hurry.

Garrett drew a deep, calming breath. *One night*, he told himself, and then this bundle of trouble would be gone, out of his life and back to St. Louis where she belonged.

It could be no other way.

CHAPTER TWO

FOR the first time in six years, Garrett was taking a woman home. He found it more than ironic that the woman in question had been someone else's intended bride, and was currently passed out on the front bench seat of his truck, her frothy, satiny wedding gown enveloping her like a shimmering cloud.

Minutes after he'd pulled out of Leisure Pointe's parking lot, without compunction or any serious thought to what she was doing, she'd stretched out, rested her head in his lap, and promptly fell asleep. Obviously, the long day she'd had, and the Amaretto she'd consumed had finally caught up to her.

That she trusted him to take care of her unsettled him. He was a complete stranger, after all. Though he'd never take advantage of a woman, he was sure if Jenna Phillips was sober and thinking clearly she never would have left Leisure Pointe with him so willingly. But considering the way she'd chosen to drown her sorrows, she'd had little choice. And as Harlan well knew, Jenna was safer with him than Beau, or even at the local motel.

The ten-minute drive to Garrett's place seemed to take thirty, and every inch of the way he tried not to think about the woman with her cheek pressed intimately against his tense thigh, but discovered he could think about little else. Her slender hand was curled just above his knee, and with every deep breath she exhaled his skin heated through the heavy denim of his jeans, electrifying his nerves. And then there was all that wild, curly hair spilling all over his lap like rich, luscious honey.

Unable to resist the temptation, he touched one of those golden strands, rubbed it between his fingers, not at all surprised to find it silky-soft, and warm as sunshine. The impulse to sink his fingers deeper into all that warmth was strong, but he didn't dare take that liberty.

Finally arriving at his two-story house, he turned into the drive and parked his truck near the front porch. A hush fell over the cab, except for Jenna's deep, even breathing. Hating to disturb her, but knowing she'd be far more comfortable once he had her in a bed, he lightly touched her bare shoulder and gave her a gentle shake.

"Jenna?" he said, keeping his voice low so as not to startle her. "C'mon, you need to get up."

Murmuring something about princes in her sleep, she rubbed her cheek against his thigh, snuggled closer to him, and sighed contentedly. He gritted his teeth as his body responded to her cuddling, ruthlessly reminding him that he'd been too long without a woman.

More determined to awaken this sleeping beauty, he gave her a firm jostling she couldn't ignore. "Wake up, Jenna."

With a groan, her lashes fluttered open, and she slowly pushed herself to a sitting position. Brushing her hair from her face, she blinked to clear her vision, then glanced from him, to the darkened house in front of them.

She frowned in confusion. "Where are we?" she

asked, her voice sleep-husky, and incredibly sexy to Garrett's ears.

Taking advantage of the reprieve, he opened his door and stepped out into the moonlit night. "We're home," he said, retrieving her one paisley-print suitcase from the bed of the truck.

He offered his hand to help her out of the vehicle, but she didn't move. Instead, she shook her head, her expression heartbreakingly bereft and desolate. "I don't have a home anymore," she whispered.

Surely she was kidding, or being extremely emotional—the latter of which made the most sense. Even if she hadn't married her fiancé, she had to live *somewhere,* have friends and family who would miss her, and a life she needed to return to soon.

"Since you can't think of anyone we can call to pick you up, you can stay here for the night. We can sort everything out in the morning, when you're feeling better." He had the sudden thought that she might be a bit apprehensive about staying at his house with him. "Are you okay with that?"

Nodding, she drew a shuddering breath and secured her hand in his, allowing him to assist her, and that mile-long train of her wedding dress out of the truck. She wobbled when both satiny shoes hit the pavement, and he automatically wrapped an arm around her waist to steady her, then ushered her toward the porch.

He helped her into his house, thankful that Chelsea had stayed at his sister's place, and that his brother had most likely found other accommodations for the night, as well. Both would be home early in the morning though, and he'd explain their extra guest then. With luck, she'd be gone before Sunday's sun set over the horizon.

He flicked on the living room lamp, giving him the illumination he needed to guide them up the stairs. Even before they arrived on the second landing, he was debating where to put her. After a quick grappling with his conscience, he decided on the most *logical* choice—his master bedroom, which had an adjoining bathroom just in case her stomach decided to rebel during the night. As for him, he'd sleep in Chelsea's bed next door.

Thanks to Chelsea, his bed was neatly made, and the clothes he normally tossed over the chair in the corner had been dropped into the hamper, giving his room a semblance of order. His little imp of a daughter was only eight, but took her chores seriously since she'd dubbed herself the "woman" of the house, though that didn't stop her from reminding him that he needed a wife, and she wanted a mom.

Unfortunately, he had no intention of marrying again. One wife had been more than enough for him and taught him a lesson he wouldn't be repeating with any woman, including this one, as enticing as she may be. As for a mom, his sister, Lisa, was a fine substitute for that maternal influence Chelsea needed.

Jenna's gaze took in his masculine furnishings without a hint of worry over whose room she might be occupying. Once she was seated on the four-poster with her wedding dress pouffed around her, he put her suitcase next to the dresser, figuring she could handle everything else on her own.

"The bathroom is right through that door," he

said, dragging his fingers through the thick, dark strands of his hair. "And if you need anything, just call for me. I'll be in the room right next to this one." He turned to go.

"Garrett?" she called softly, halting him before he could make a quick escape.

He exhaled heavily and glanced back at her, instantly steeling himself against that lost look in her eyes. "Yeah?"

Her satiny pumps hit the floor as she toed them off one at a time. "I...I can't undo the buttons on my dress by myself."

She slid back to her feet, turned around, and gathered her luxurious hair over her shoulder, presenting him with a row of at least two dozen pearl buttons that started between her shoulder blades and marched all the way down to the curve of her bottom.

He stood there, paralyzed by the thought of helping her to undress. His first instinct was to tell her to sleep in the gown, but knew that suggestion was ridiculous. She had to be extremely uncomfortable, and she had to get out of the gown sooner or later.

Resigned to the inevitable, he came up behind her. With hands that were none too steady, he fumbled with the small, slippery buttons, unable to ignore the ever-widening expanse of smooth, pale skin he revealed. As the material loosened, she crossed her arms over her chest, holding it in place. She wore what looked like a white, satin corset, and he unhooked that, too, knowing she'd never be able to do it on her own.

Finally, he completed the intimate task just as the lacy band of her panties came into view. He stepped back, wanting to bolt from the room, from his tempting reaction to this woman, but realized that she seemed unsure of what to do next, or how to step out of the bulk of her wedding dress without getting tangled up in the yards of heavy material.

She looked to him for help—and the next step was getting her into something she could sleep in for the night.

He stifled a groan. Not wanting to take the time to sort through the garments in her suitcase and possibly end up with something flimsy and more befitting a honeymoon night, he grabbed one of his chambray shirts from his closets and thrust it toward her. Gratitude filled her eyes, and as soon as her fingers curled around the soft material, he turned around, giving her privacy to change.

A minute later she said softly, "I'm done."

He turned to face her again, relieved to find all the important, voluptuous parts of her decently covered—though he couldn't help but appreciate how well she filled out his large shirt. Her unbound breasts were full and high, grazing the soft, faded cotton. The hem flirted around her slender thighs, drawing his gaze to those long, graceful legs of hers covered in ivory stockings, prompting fantasies he had no business imagining.

Awareness rumbled through him, settling in his belly like hot coals. Needing the distraction, he helped her from the crumpled dress, then pulled down the covers and gave the firm mattress a pat.

"In you go," he said lightly, the words echoing his nightly routine with his daughter.

The very grown-up woman with centerfold curves sat on his bed, but before he could yank the covers up to her chin, she glanced down at her legs dangling over the side of the mattress. "My stockings and garter," she murmured, a perplexed frown creasing her brow. "I can't sleep with them on. I want them off."

Garrett's jaw clenched with restraint. He'd been hoping she wouldn't notice her stockings, and he was willing to bet that as soon as her head hit the pillow she'd be out like a light and nothing would disturb her, not even that extra lingerie. But there was a sudden stubborn glint in her eye that told him his torment wasn't over. He stepped back to let her do the deed, and crossed his arms over his chest so he wouldn't be tempted to help. Without modesty, she hiked up the hem of his shirt and reached down, swaying off balance. She managed to catch herself, just barely, before she toppled over.

Her tenacity would have amused him if she didn't arouse him so much.

For a sober woman, the task should have been a simple one, and possibly even a provocative striptease. For a woman who was all thumbs and couldn't get those thumbs tucked beneath the band of her stockings, the deed was a monumental one. Her frustration mounted as her fingers slipped, and a choked sound escaped her. When she glanced up at him, hopeless tears brimmed in her eyes, turning them to a velvet shade of blue.

She bit her trembling bottom lip in a valiant attempt to hold her emotions at bay. "I can't do anything right today."

If she hadn't looked so beaten, he might have been able to resist the silent plea in her gaze. This was no calculated attempt to seduce him as he'd come to expect from most women, but a raw, honest need for his assistance.

Breaking his vow not to touch her, he brushed her hands away and hooked his fingers into the lacy band of her stocking with as much indifference as he could muster. His mind managed to remain detached from the situation, but when the calloused pads of his fingers accidently stroked her silky, delicate skin on the way down her leg, his body burned with a long denied hunger.

Irritated with his response to this woman, he finished the intimate task quickly. "Lie down and get some sleep," he ordered in a gruff tone, anxious to get out of his bedroom.

She eased back on the pillows, her hair floating around her head like a halo of gold. Her expression softened as she blinked up at him slumberously. Glancing away, he lifted the covers beneath her arms and tucked her in. Just when he would have straightened and turned to go, she grabbed his shirt, holding him inches above her.

Heart pounding, he waited to see what she intended to do.

A multitude of emotions shifted across her face, too many to pinpoint just one. "Garrett," she said, the drowsiness stealing over her making her voice husky and warm. "Thank you."

Her lips were inches away, inviting and lush, and that sexy beauty mark beckoned to him. Had he ever wanted something so badly as to settle his mouth over Jenna's and taste her?

He swallowed, hard. "For what?" he managed, his voice low and raspy.

"For taking care of me." An achingly tender

smile curved her mouth. "It's been so long since anyone has been so kind to me, so caring."

Garrett tried to straighten to break the physical and mental hold she'd seemed to cast over him, but couldn't move. He felt himself being inexorably pulled toward her, not by the strength of her hands fisted in his shirt, but by his own damnable weakness, and the lure of what her soft, parted lips might offer.

Sweetness. Surrender. And a passion he suddenly craved more than his next breath.

He never meant for the kiss to happen. Never meant to allow himself to get caught up in needs and desires he'd buried long ago. But when she slowly slid one hand up around the back of his neck and into the hair curling over the collar of his shirt, then brought his mouth to hers, his senses spun. Her lashes fluttered closed, and resisting her became a distant thought. A Herculean effort he didn't have the strength to battle.

The gesture itself was chaste enough, an expression of gratitude, he knew, but the way her lips molded so perfectly to his made the embrace seem more sensual than an overtly provocative kiss. Her mouth was warm and incredibly plush beneath his, so giving and sweet.

So full of the kind of promises he stopped believing in long ago.

Slowly, reluctantly, he pulled back. She made a token sound of protest as their lips drew apart, but her hands fell away and her eyes never opened. Giving in to the exhaustion he knew she'd been fighting, she settled back into his pillow. With a soft, dreamy sigh she drifted off to sleep, leaving Garrett to wonder if she'd remember any of this in the morning.

Probably not.

Hopefully not.

With a groan that seemed to reverberate through Jenna's aching head, she rolled to her side and pried her eyes open against the sunlight filtering into the room...and stared into the face of a pretty little girl with long, straight blond hair Jenna instantly envied, inquisitive green eyes, and a contemplative expression. The girl was on her knees at the side of the bed, elbows propped on the mattress, and her chin bracketed between her palms, as if she'd been there for a while, waiting for Jenna to wake up.

"Why are you sleeping in my daddy's bed?" she asked, more curious than accusing.

Not recognizing the girl and startled by her question, Jenna's heart leapt in her chest as she frantically searched her disoriented, foggy memory, trying to remember where she was, and how she'd gotten in this strange room and this large bed that seemed to envelop her in a subtle, masculine scent she recognized as belonging to the prince who'd rescued her last night.

Jenna squeezed her eyes shut. *Last night,* and the devastating events that led to her fleeing to a town where no one knew her flooded her memory like a tidal wave. She'd been so overwhelmed by shame that she'd leapt into the limousine waiting to take her and Sheldon to the country club for their reception, and hysterically ordered the chauffeur to *Just drive!* She hadn't cared to where, just so long as she put as many miles as she could between her and the disgraceful past she couldn't seem to escape. A past that would forever haunt her. A past that marred her chances of ever being respected, or respectable. What made her believe she could fit in to Sheldon's affluent life and be the wife to a prominent surgeon? She'd tried to conform, but she couldn't erase the mistake she'd made. His well-to-do family and their elite circle of friends weren't willing to dismiss what she'd done, either.

An hour outside of St. Louis, in the small town of Danby, the annoyed limo driver had pulled into the parking lot of Leisure Pointe and informed her that he hadn't been paid to take her on a trek across Missouri. Knowing there was nothing left for her in St. Louis, she'd climbed out of the limousine, entered the rowdy establishment, and sank despondently into a booth in a far corner—feeling more heavy-hearted and isolated than ever.

She remembered faceless men sending Amaretto her way. She remembered the bartender keeping those same hounds at bay when it was obvious she wanted to be left alone. She remembered *Garrett*, with his deep, dark blue eyes, and the way he'd made her feel safe and secure when she'd believed she'd never feel safe and secure again.

Her hand fluttered to her lips, and her belly tumbled, not from the aftereffects of consuming too much Amaretto, but from something far more pleasant, and far more frightening. Most of all, she remembered kissing her gorgeous, raven-haired prince and the sweet, tender acceptance that had filled her in that fleeting moment.

And then she remembered nothing as deep sleep consumed her. Jenna felt a gentle tug on her hair, prompting her to leave her private thoughts behind and lift her lashes to deal with her unexpected visitor. The little girl had a strand of Jenna's hair corkscrewed around her finger, seemingly fascinated with the way it clung so naturally.

"How come you're sleeping in my daddy's bed?" she asked again, more insistent this time.

Still absorbing the surprise of finding a pixie watching over her, she chose her answer carefully. "Well, I needed a place to sleep for the night, and your daddy let me use his bed." That much she remembered.

"Oh." Her little nose scrunched up as she thought about that. "And you're wearing his shirt, too."

She glanced down, confirming that the nightshirt she wore wasn't the silky chemise she'd packed for her honeymoon. More memories tumbled through her foggy mind, of Garrett helping her to undress, and the intensity in his deep blue eyes...

The little imp tilted her head to the side. "What's your name?"

"Jenna." She offered a small smile. "What's yours?"

"Chelsea Blackwell." Pushing away from the bed, she strolled over to the froth of satin draped over the chair in the corner of the room and stroked her hand over the shimmery material. "This is like a fairy princess dress," she said in awe.

Too bad her dreams hadn't come true like they did in fairy tales, Jenna thought, unable to fend off the sharp sting of disappointment she experienced. "It's a wedding dress," she said in a tight, achy voice.

"Did my daddy marry you?" Chelsea glanced back at Jenna, her green, guileless eyes round with hope. "Are you my new mom?"

Jenna immediately shook her head to ward off the child's line of questioning. "No, your dad didn't marry me, honey, and I'm not your new mom." Gingerly sitting up, she swung her legs over the edge of the bed and waited for her head to stop spinning. She hated bursting the little girl's bubble of excitement, and offered the only consolation that came to mind. "But I'd like to be your friend."

"Okay." Seemingly satisfied with that compromise, Chelsea grinned, revealing a dimple in her right cheek. "Does that mean you're staying here?"

Jenna honestly didn't know what she was going to do, and hoped over the next few weeks she'd be able to figure out which direction her life would now take. No matter her decision, she doubted it encompassed staying in this house with Garrett and this adorable little girl.

Before she could formulate a response, booted steps echoed up the stairs, then her prince from last night entered the room. In the light of day, and without any alcohol to impair her brain or vision, she came to the stunning conclusion that he was even more gorgeous than she recalled. Dressed in faded jeans that molded to his lean hips and a casual shirt that was fitted to a nicely muscled chest, he exuded a rugged masculinity that was a sharp contrast to the preppie, button-down image Sheldon and his friends preferred. This man was earthy and physical, with jet-black hair that set off his striking blue eyes, and a sensually cut mouth that made him all the more breathtaking and much too appealing.

Though his demeanor was reserved and distant, his warm gaze swept over her, taking in her disheveled hair, and making her all too aware that she was wearing *his* shirt. His eyes lingered briefly on her bare legs, prompting restless memories of him removing her stockings, and his hands caressing her skin.

Then he glanced toward Chelsea. A smiled curved his lips, softening his expression and captivating Jenna even more.

"Hey, there you are, pup," he said, his deep voice rich with affection. "I wondered where you'd disappeared to."

"I came in here to make your bed and found Jenna sleeping in it." She hurried over to her father, clasped her hands together beneath her chin, and looked up at him beseechingly. "Can she stay with us? Pretty please?"

"She's not a stray pet for you to keep," he said with gentle humor. "Jenna only needed a place to stay for the night, and I'm sure now that she's rested, she'll be heading back home." He tapped a finger beneath Chelsea's chin. "Why don't you go downstairs to the kitchen and I'll be there in a few minutes to make breakfast."

Chelsea did as she was told, and once she was gone, the room filled with silence. Jenna's gaze connected with Garrett's, and her stomach fluttered, not with nausea, but an awareness that took her completely off guard. The last thing she needed to deal with was this unexpected attraction to a man she barely knew, not when she was trying to come to terms with everything that had happened yesterday, along with her uncertain future.

She drew a stabilizing breath. "I take it 'pup' is your daughter?"

He nodded, and rubbed a hand along the back of his neck, looking uncomfortable now that they were alone. "Yeah, she's mine," he replied, an odd, possessive note to his voice. "I call her pup because ever since she took her first step she's followed me around like a puppy."

It wasn't difficult to imagine Chelsea tagging along behind her father. Though Garrett's parental love was unmistakable, and his daughter's devotion just as strong, there was no physical resemblance between the two. His pitch-black hair and vivid blue eyes were an obvious contrast to Chelsea's blond hair, green eyes, and fair, enchanting features.

"Chelsea must look like her mother," she said, speaking her thoughts out loud and attempting to make idle conversation.

Her comment startled him, and his dark brows drew into a frown. "No, not really," he muttered.

His curt tone didn't invite further discussion of Chelsea's mother, and Jenna decided the best course of action would be to steer clear of the subject, which appeared to be a touchy one. "Well, your daughter is sweet, and adorable. And very precocious. She thought you and I got married."

He visibly winced, but remained across the room, keeping an appropriate amount of distance between them. "Chelsea's mom died when she was barely two, so she doesn't remember much about her, and lately she's been asking for a mother. I suppose seeing your wedding dress and finding you in my bedroom led her to the wrong conclusion."

"It was a very hopeful conclusion," she said

softly, understanding the little girl's need to replace her missing parent. Jenna had grown up never knowing her father, and though her mother had been a good single parent despite their struggles, she'd never had a dependable male influence in her life, and that was a loss she still felt.

"Well, it's best that she doesn't entertain those kinds of thoughts, and I don't encourage them, either," he replied meaningfully. "How are you feeling?" he asked, smoothly and effectively changing the topic once again.

"A little fuzzy, but overall okay, all things considered." She dragged her fingers through her tousled hair, feeling contrite for disrupting his life, even for one day. "Garrett...I'm very sorry about last night."

"There's nothing to apologize for." He shrugged those broad shoulders of his. "You weren't in any shape to go anywhere and I gave you a place to stay."

"No doubt I ruined your evening. I intruded on your home life and family, and I even slept in your bed. And from the bits and pieces that I can remember, I know I made a fool of myself at the bar."

She recalled babbling on about silly things like hating her curly hair and making wishes to marry her own prince charming and living happily ever after—not that Garrett would understand the hopes and dreams she'd carried with her since childhood.

She ducked her head, and absently toyed with the hem of the shirt she wore. "And contrary to my behavior last night, I'm not in the habit of kissing strangers."

Except Garrett hadn't felt like a stranger. He'd

been warm and receptive, and no matter how wrong, she found it difficult to regret that sweet, tender kiss, which had made her feel so safe and secure. There had been no pretenses, no expectations, just the kind of acceptance she'd craved for so long.

And Garrett probably thought she was a brazen hussy for allowing such liberties just hours after leaving her groom at the altar.

Shaking her head of those thoughts, she lifted her gaze back to his. "I *am* sorry about that kiss," she said softly.

"No, I'm the one who should apologize." Though his tone held a gruff certainty, his irises had taken on a dark, sensual shade of blue that belied his attempt at disinterest. "It won't happen again."

He sounded so determined, Jenna couldn't help but wonder if maybe, possibly, he'd been just as affected by that kiss as she'd been.

The moment was shattered by the front door slamming shut, and someone bounding up the stairs. "Honey, I'm home!" a deep, masculine voice called out, his tone laced with carefree humor.

Jenna's gaze widened in surprise, and Garrett groaned, pressing his fingers to the bridge of his nose. A good-looking man briefly glanced inside Garrett's room as he passed, then the heavy steps came to an abrupt stop, and he backed up, filling the doorway with his presence.

The man, who looked like a slightly younger version of her prince—albeit more tousled—glanced from Jenna, to Garrett, and grinned. "Well, I'll be damned, big brother. Looks like I wasn't the only one who got lucky last night."

Jenna's face warmed at the insinuation, and

Garrett grimaced. "This isn't what you think, Rylan," he quickly corrected.

Rylan's dark brows rose incredulously. "You mean to tell me you had a beautiful woman in your bed and you didn't—"

Garrett held up a hand, effectively cutting him off with the gesture and the warning look he shot his way. "No, we *didn't*, and I'll explain everything downstairs."

The other man didn't budge. "Don't I even get an introduction?"

Garrett sighed, the sound rife with impatience. "Jenna, this is my younger brother, Rylan. Ry, Jenna Phillips."

"It's nice to meet you," she said, finding the other man amusing, and not nearly as serious as his older sibling.

"Likewise." He scrutinized her face, making her feel self-conscious. "You're not from around here, are you?"

"No, she's from St. Louis," Garrett replied before she could respond, then headed toward his brother to usher him out of the room. "And she won't be around long enough for you to start flirting with."

"To heck with flirting," he said with a gregarious grin and a wink at Jenna. "I was going to jump right to asking her out on a date."

Garrett's expression turned surprisingly fierce. "Tired of Emma Gentry so soon?"

Rylan shrugged. "Emma and I aren't exclusive."

"And Jenna isn't interested," Garrett countered, pointing toward the door. "Out, Ry."

Jenna bit back a chuckle at the good-natured bickering, and the fact that Garrett felt the need to protect her virtue from his fun-loving, but womanizing brother.

Once Rylan was out of the room, Garrett turned back to her and said wryly, "Welcome to the crazy Blackwell household. As you might have guessed, having a female guest in the house, and especially in my bedroom, is a novelty."

Though he'd injected humor into his voice, his comment said a lot about Garrett, himself—that he was a man of integrity, which he'd proved by rescuing her last night and giving her a safe place to sleep, and he was very discreet when it came to his family and personal life. She appreciated those qualities, even as she realized just how much her indiscreet past would clash with his admirable values.

The thought of embroiling Garrett and his family in the scandal that would forever nip at her heels brought reality crashing down around her. Despite enjoying the Blackwells's warmth and friendliness, the last thing she wanted to do was take advantage of their hospitality.

She drew a breath that did nothing to dispel the ache in her chest, and slid off the bed. "I'd like to take a shower and change, if that's okay." At his nod, she smiled and added, "I'll be downstairs just as soon as I'm presentable."

"Breakfast will be waiting." He backed toward the bedroom door, but not before giving her bare legs one last warm lingering glance she felt as strongly as his touch last night.

Then he was gone.

CHAPTER THREE

BREAKFAST wasn't the only thing waiting for Jenna downstairs in the kitchen. She came to an abrupt stop when she found herself alone with a pretty, but very pregnant woman who was in the process of clearing the table. One look at her striking blue eyes and straight, glossy black hair that brushed her shoulders, and she was fairly certain she'd just encountered another Blackwell.

The other woman wasn't shocked to find a strange woman in the house, but her kind gaze did a quick head-to-toe inventory of Jenna's blue linen short outfit and matching heeled sandals, which obviously were not the kind of attire suited to a relaxing Sunday around the house. But, the outfit had been one her fiancé had selected, and was the most casual thing she'd packed for their honeymoon because she knew Sheldon preferred she always dress stylishly and looked the height of sophistication.

She suddenly felt like a fraud. The woman wearing the fashionable outfit was who she'd tried so desperately to be for Sheldon's sake, and even on some level for her mother. But the glaring truth remained. Beneath the fancy trappings, Jenna was a plain and simple woman, and she suddenly wanted to be accepted for who and what she was, without pretenses, and without being judged by her past mistake—*if* that was even possible.

"Good morning," the other woman greeted her,

smiling amicably as she set the dishes she was carrying into the sink. "Would you like some coffee, or breakfast? Garrett left you a plate of pancakes warming in the oven if you're hungry."

Though her head had cleared from her shower, the thought of food made Jenna's stomach tumble. "Maybe in a little bit. Just coffee for now, thank you."

She watched the woman bring a mug down from the cupboard and pour steaming liquid into the cup then motion to the ceramic containers next to the pot. "Help yourself to cream and sugar."

Jenna came up to the counter and sweetened her coffee. "Where's Garrett?" she asked curiously, having expected her host to be in the kitchen.

"He's outside with Rylan and my husband, Duane, poking around under the hood of our truck to check out a problem with the water pump. He'll be back up to the house anytime. And Chelsea is playing out back." She rested her hand on the swell of her very large belly. "And since I can see that you're wondering who I am, I'm Lisa, Garrett's sister."

"It's nice to meet you," she replied, shaking Lisa's offered hand. "I'm Jenna Phillips, but I'm assuming you already knew that."

"Yes. Garrett told us why you're here and what happened last night at Leisure Pointe."

Surprisingly, there wasn't any judgment or criticism in Lisa's tone, but Jenna was certain the other woman was wondering why she'd run out on her groom on her wedding day. An explanation was complicated, and the humiliation and shame that accompanied her reasons wasn't something she wished to discuss with anyone.

She returned to stirring her coffee. "Considering my frame of mind yesterday, I appreciate his kindness in taking me in for the night."

"Yeah, well, it's nice to see that my brother is still capable of doing a noble deed for a woman when the situation calls for it," Lisa said wryly.

Jenna followed Lisa to the kitchen table with her coffee, and took a seat on one of the pine chairs. She found Lisa's comment ambiguous and odd, with an underlying intimation she couldn't quite grasp. For as hospitable as Garrett had been to her last night, and despite his *noble deed,* their earlier conversation had given her the distinct impression that he fully expected her to be on her way back *home* today. Unfortunately, there wasn't anything left for her in St. Louis, unless bad memories and a sense of failure counted for anything.

Taking a sip of her coffee, she dropped her gaze to Lisa's pregnant belly and changed the subject. "When are you due?"

Lisa gingerly lowered herself onto one of the chairs next to Jenna's. "Not soon enough." She laughed, and Jenna did, too. "I'm having twins, and they aren't due for another four or five weeks, according to my last doctor's appointment, but I feel like Jacob and Janet are ready to make their debut into the world *now.*"

"Twins, and a boy and a girl at that," Jenna marveled, tucking a springy, loose curl behind her ear. "How wonderful."

Lisa rubbed her stomach lovingly, though exhaustion lined her features. "Yeah, it is wonderful, but I have to admit, the thought of having two at once is very intimidating.''

Despite those legitimate fears, Jenna envied the other woman and the family of her own she'd have very soon. That was something she'd wished for herself, had hoped would happen with Sheldon, but she'd forfeited that particular dream when she'd left him at the altar—and he'd done nothing to stop her from leaving.

She cleared the sudden tightness from her throat. ''I'm sure maternal instincts will kick in and you'll be fine.''

''That's what I keep telling myself, too.'' Lisa shifted in her seat, her bulky girth seemingly making it difficult to find a comfortable position.

A few minutes later, Garrett finally entered the kitchen. His gaze landed on Jenna first, and he took in her sophisticated short suit and heeled shoes with a combination of interest and mild scrutiny before glancing at his sister.

''The water pump is temporarily fixed until you can get the truck in for repair this week,'' he told her, heading to the sink to wash his hands. ''Duane is waiting for you outside, and he's ready to go. Thank you for watching Chelsea last night.''

''It was my pleasure. She's a joy to have over, you know that.'' Lisa struggled to stand, and Garrett was immediately at her side, gently grasping her arm to help her up. Once she was steady on her feet, she laughed breathlessly. ''All three of us thank you for your assistance.'' She pressed a hand to the base of her spine. ''I'll see you at the office tomorrow.''

''I'll be there early,'' he replied. ''I have an estimate to work on and I won't be heading into the city to check on the Leiberman project until eleven. Since there's nothing pressing going on in the morning, take your time getting there."

"I'll be there early, too," she said, reaching for her purse. "I've got a stack of payables that need to be entered into the computer and—" An unexpected "oomph" cut Lisa off midsentence. Her hand shot to her lower belly, and she grimaced at the discomfort her babies had caused.

Garrett's mouth thinned into a tight line. "I think it's past time you went on maternity leave. You should be at home resting, not at the office working."

She caressed a soothing hand over her abdomen. "The doctor said I can work right up until the babies are born if I feel up to it."

"And I'm your older brother and boss and I say that if you don't take the paid leave that you're due, then I'm going to have to fire you." His tone was half-joking, but his expression was completely serious. "You're into your eighth month, and you look exhausted. I'll put an ad in the local paper this week for a secretary to handle the filing and basic front-end office work. And no more watching Chelsea in the afternoons after day camp. While you're on leave, she can stay with me at the office."

She rolled her eyes at his protectiveness and concern. "You're being ridiculous, Garrett."

"That's my prerogative," he said, though the affection creasing his expression softened his rebuke. "Take advantage of what little time you have left to yourself, sis, because life as you know it will never be the same once those two are born."

Lisa opened her mouth to argue, but Jenna

watched with a small degree of amusement as
Garrett cut off her debate with a stern look that silently told his sister she couldn't hope to sway his
opinion.

"Fine. You win," she relented with a sigh, then
turned toward Jenna with a weary grin. "It was very
nice meeting you."

"You, too." Jenna returned the smile, feeling as
though she'd made a friend in Lisa. "Good luck
with those twins."

As soon as Lisa was gone, Garrett reverted back
to the reserved, emotionally guarded man who'd left
her upstairs earlier. Grabbing a mug from the cupboard, he poured himself a cup of the darkened brew
then held the pot her way. "Do you need a warm-
up?"

"Sure. Half a cup will be fine."

He crossed the kitchen and refilled her mug.
Standing so close, she caught the warm, masculine
scent that was uniquely his, and was all too aware
of the steady trip of her pulse. Everything about the
man made her senses come alive, and she found the
unfamiliar sensation both exciting and disconcert-
ing.

With effort, she shook off the feeling. The last
thing she wanted or needed was the complication of
being attracted to Garrett Blackwell, no matter how
gorgeous and sexually appealing he was, when her
priorities lay in figuring out the direction of her future first.

He set the coffeepot back on the burner and retrieved the platter of pancakes he'd left warming in
the oven. "Did you eat breakfast?"

Her stomach had calmed, but she wasn't certain she was ready for food. "I'm really not hungry."

He slanted her one of those uncompromising looks he'd just used on his sister. "You need something other than coffee before you leave."

"I'm fine," she insisted.

"What did you have to eat yesterday?" He crossed his arms over that wide chest of his, looking ruggedly male. "I'm assuming you ran out on your wedding before you had the chance to enjoy your reception or dinner."

The slight censure in his voice caused her to straighten defensively in her seat. "I had half a sandwich for lunch. I was nervous and couldn't eat much more than that."

"Well, Amaretto and coffee isn't going to get you very far." He forked one of the golden brown pancakes onto a plate, and brought it to her at the table. "Try at least a few bites. And while you're eating, we can figure out what we're going to do with you."

"What *we're* going to do with me?" She slathered a thin layer of butter onto the pancake and added a stream of syrup. "Between *that* comment and the one you made earlier to Chelsea, I *am* beginning to feel like a stray pet." She met his gaze steadily, not wanting him to feel duty-bound to be her guardian. "I appreciate what you did for me last night and giving me a place to stay, but you aren't responsible for what happens to me, Garrett."

"You became my responsibility the moment I told Harlan I'd take you home for the night," he refuted gruffly.

She was at once touched by his chivalrous sentiment, and startled by the deeper layer of resentment she detected in his tone. He might be a man of integrity, but for a reason unknown to her it was very apparent that last night's arrangement hadn't thrilled him, along with the misplaced sense of obligation he felt toward her this morning. And she was fairly certain she'd compounded his burden with that spontaneous kiss she'd given him just before she'd fallen into a deep sleep.

Though her mind had been fuzzy from liquor, exhaustion and regrets, she clearly recalled the sensual way his lips had molded to hers and the provocative sweetness of his response.

There hadn't been an ounce of reservation between them during that fleeting embrace, which now contradicted the tense demeanor of the man standing a few feet away from her.

"Why did you do it?" she asked quietly. "Bring me home with you, I mean. You could have left me at Leisure Pointe to fend for myself."

He scoffed at that. "Sweetheart, you were far from being able to take care of yourself. You were in no shape to be left alone, and your options were limited. I couldn't see you spending the night in a holding cell, and I wasn't about to let Beau Harding *accompany* you to a motel. I was your safest bet."

"Thank you."

He shrugged off her gratitude. Leaning a hip against the counter, he took a sip of his coffee, his vivid, breathtaking blue eyes studying her from over the rim. "So, what do you plan on doing now?"

"You mean now that I'm no longer someone's bride?" she asked, knowing that's what his question implied. "I honestly don't know." She had no real direction, just the overwhelming need to be true to herself, to embrace the freedom and independence that was now hers. "I'm hoping to figure out the answer to that question one step at a time."

And her first order of business was to buy herself casual, comfortable clothes. The kind she used to wear, before her mother insisted she become a lady and secure herself a respectable husband. A sophisticated outfit might give her the appearance of elegance and refinement, but it couldn't cover up a tainted past. And she'd feel more like herself in T-shirts, jeans, and simple cotton dresses.

Stabbing a slice of pancake with her fork, she dragged the piece through a thick pool of maple syrup. "Is there a thrift store around here?"

His gaze flickered over her classy, citified attire, and a slight, confused frown marred his dark brows. "A thrift store?" he echoed, his surprise evident in his tone.

"Yes." Considering her personal finances were very limited, she'd have to watch her spending habits. "There's a few things I need, and a secondhand store will do just fine."

"Well, there's Kate's Korner," he offered, still sounding uncertain that's what she wanted. "Her place is located down on Mulberry Avenue."

"Perfect." She ate another bite of her breakfast, finding the pancake amazingly good and filling.

Still frowning and appearing confused, he set his mug in the sink and rubbed a hand across the back of his neck. "I'll have Rylan take you to Kate's if that's what you'd like, then back to the city."

Obviously, he was anxious to be rid of her, not that she could blame him after the way she'd disrupted his life. But one thing she knew for certain—

she wasn't going back to St. Louis, not when the life she'd led there had all been an illusion, filled with expectations she couldn't hope to live up to. Not anymore.

"That's not necessary—having Rylan take me back to St. Louis, that is." She pulled in a deep breath, exhaled slowly, and embraced her decision. "I'm thinking of staying here in Danby for a while."

Disbelief flashed across his handsome features. *"Why?"* The one word escaped him on a strangled note of shock and incredulity.

She set her fork down on her plate, and dabbed at the corner of her mouth with her napkin. "There isn't anything left for me in St. Louis," she said simply. "Not anymore."

He stared at her for a long moment. "What about your family?"

She remembered bits and pieces of their conversation at Leisure Pointe the night before. "I told you that I don't have any family, and that's true," she said softly. "I never knew my father, I don't have any siblings, and my mother died three years ago of emphysema."

"What about grandparents, or aunts, or uncles, or other relatives? There has to be *someone.*"

"I never knew any of them." Not wanting to dredge up her family history, and just how unsupportive her grandparents had been when Jenna's mother had gotten pregnant with her at the young age of seventeen, she stood and took her dish to the sink. "There really is *no one.*"

"What about your fiancé?" Garrett asked, sounding near desperate to find someone willing to come and take her back to St. Louis. "I'm sure whatever happened between the two of you can be worked out somehow."

Her chest tightened unexpectedly. Resuming her relationship with Sheldon was impossible, she knew. She planned to call him later today to apologize and make sure he knew just how sorry she was for embroiling him and his family in the middle of her own personal scandal, and she had no doubt that the conversation would put an end to them as a couple.

She ducked her head and rinsed her plate and utensils, giving the task more attention than it warranted. Anything to avoid Garrett's penetrating gaze. "Things are definitely over between Sheldon and I."

"Didn't you love him?"

There was that censure again, and because Garrett didn't know the reasons why she'd run out on her wedding day, she couldn't blame him for expressing a bit of criticism. Judging by his tone, he most likely believed she was a flighty female who'd broken her fiancé's heart.

"I cared about Sheldon. Very much." He was a good, decent man, and though they'd spoken of love, it had never been the kind of all-consuming, passionate emotion that she'd dreamed of. "But going our separate ways is for the best."

Feeling restless under Garrett's scrutiny, she kept her gaze averted, looking out the window over the sink. He had a big backyard that was immaculately landscaped and maintained, with a swimming pool that dominated the area. The sun shimmered off the water, inviting relief from the heat of summer.

Beyond that, she caught a glimpse of Chelsea as she played on a sturdy, wooden swing set.

"You'll go back to St. Louis, Jenna," Garrett said, his voice infused with certainty. "That's where you live."

Yes, she'd *lived* there, but she'd never truly belonged in that big, overwhelming city. "I don't live there any longer, Garrett." Drying her hands on a dish towel, she finally turned his way to look at him. "And despite what you want to believe, there is no reason for me to go back."

He opened his mouth to issue an argument, and she promptly cut him off with irrefutable proof of having no ties left to the city. "I quit my secretarial job last month to be a stay-at-home wife for Sheldon. I didn't renew my lease on my apartment because I wasn't going to need it, and Sheldon had me sell my car and he bought me a Mercedes sedan that he felt was more suitable for a doctor's wife." She ticked each point off on her fingers for emphasis. "All the personal belongings I have were packed in a few boxes, which I'm sure Sheldon will be more than happy to forward to my new address, whatever it may be."

Her voice cracked with unexpected emotion, but she forced herself to finish, for Garrett's sake as much as her own. "Until I figure out what I'm going to do with my life, and my future, staying here in Danby is just as good a place as any."

His jaw clenched tight, but he said nothing, seemingly taken aback by her outburst.

"I get the distinct impression that you don't want me here, but I'm staying," she went on, intent on setting him straight on all accounts and trying to maintain her dignity in the process. "I'm sure I've caused you enough trouble after last night, but once I leave your house, consider your obligation to me over and done with. The last thing I want is to be a burden to *anyone*."

They stared at one another, their gazes locked in a silent contest of wills. The tension in the kitchen was so tangible it nearly crackled in the space of air separating them. Garrett drew slow, deep breaths, amazed at how the gold rimming her eyes glowed with heat and the fiery spirit she'd displayed. Her back was ramrod-straight in her elegant attire, her posture filled with pride, but there was no denying the vulnerability lurking beneath that tough facade.

As the seconds ticked on the clock on the wall next to him, in equally slow increments guilt trickled through Garrett, easing the agitation that had pulled the muscles taut across his shoulders during her spiel. *Aw, hell,* he thought as his body gradually relaxed. He'd provoked her, and he deserved every bit of her upbraiding.

Analyzing his reasons for pushing her was ridiculously easy. She *was* a burden, the kind that wreaked havoc with his senses and his libido, and on some distant level, his emotions. And that's what irked him most of all—his attraction to her when she was exactly the kind of distraction he didn't need in his life.

He didn't want Jenna here in Danby for those purely selfish reasons, yet it appeared that he had little choice in the matter. All he could do was accept the inevitable and wait out her decision to stay. She might not return to St. Louis, but he found it unlikely that she'd choose Danby as her permanent home. Other than the residents that lived here all their lives, there was little to keep a visitor interested in the small community.

His own wife had proved that theory and had quickly grown bored with the quaint charm of the town, and he'd paid dearly for Angela's lack of interest in their marriage and the baby daughter she'd borne.

The reminder of his dead wife's betrayal pulled everything back into perspective for Garrett. Just like Angela, Jenna had shunned commitment and ties in favor of independence and freedom, and though he didn't know the exact reasons why Jenna had run out on her wedding, her unwillingness to work through whatever problems she'd encountered with her bridegroom was enough to convince Garrett that this woman's time in Danby was temporary, until something better and more exciting came along.

He exhaled a resigned breath of air. "If you're staying in Danby, then I guess I ought to get used to the two of us running into each other."

"Yes, I suppose you should." Her chin lifted a fraction, revealing a stubborn side to her personality he at once admired and begrudged. Her hair rippled with the movement, an untamable cascade of curls that beckoned to him like a bright, golden halo. Without thinking of the consequences, and forgetting the lecture he'd just given himself, he lifted his hand and gently tucked a wayward curl behind her ear, but the rebellious strand sprang back to taunt him. He let his fingers glide across her soft cheek, then stroked his thumb over that sensual beauty mark dotting the left side of her mouth. She drew a shuddering breath and gazed up at him with eyes filled with uncertainty, and a longing that tugged at something deep and vital within him.

He told himself to back away, to leave her alone. But then he remembered how sweet she'd tasted last night, and all logic fled, replaced by a hunger and need that warred with his conscience and the voice in his head warning him to let her, and this fleeting moment, go.

He wanted to taste her again, and he was helpless to deny the irresistible, tantalizing pull between them.

Seemingly struck mute by his unexpected touch, she didn't protest when he slipped his hand around to the nape of her neck and used his thumb to tip her chin up higher, though her eyes widened in wary surprise. Her lips parted, but not to issue an objection. No, she seemed incapable of speech, but her actions were completely in sync with his.

Despite their differences and the argument they'd just engaged in, she wanted him, too. Anticipation swirled between them, and he lowered his head... just as the front door slammed shut.

Jenna jumped back, breaking the hold he'd had on her, and he instantly let her go, realizing just how far he'd nearly taken things between them. Further than he'd intended, that's for sure! He had no business touching her so intimately, let alone indulging in another kiss with her.

Her cheeks were flushed pink, and her eyes reflected shock and dismay at her own behavior. She swallowed, apparently to find her voice, but before she could utter a word Rylan entered the kitchen.

Jenna was so grateful for Rylan's sudden appearance she could have wept with appreciation, especially when she'd done nothing to discourage Garrett's advance, or the kiss they'd been tumbling toward.

What was wrong with her? Without Rylan's interruption, she no doubt would have allowed Garrett to sweep her up into the maelstrom of awareness that seemingly rippled between them—a dangerous, reckless kind of attraction she wasn't prepared to handle, no matter how desirable and feminine he made her feel.

She wasn't staying in Danby to compound her mistakes, and she definitely wasn't looking for any kind of involvement with a man—no matter how much *he* enticed her. She had too many issues to resolve, and a deep, dark secret no man would be happy to discover.

She transferred her gaze to Rylan and summoned a smile that felt stiff on her lips. Speculation shone in his eyes, and a grin curved his mouth, but he declined to comment on the obvious undercurrents in the room.

Instead, he shifted his attention to his brother. "I'm heading to the hardware store to pick up fertilizer for the front lawn," he told Garrett. "I thought I'd check and see if you needed anything while I'm in town."

Garrett shook his head and shoved his hands into the front pockets of his jeans—the same hands that had caressed her skin so tenderly moments ago. "No, but you can take Jenna with you when you leave."

"Oh?" The one word held a wealth of curiosity. Garrett subtly moved toward the table, putting distance between them. "She wants to get a few things from Kate's Korner."

"And if you can recommend a place for me to stay, I'd appreciate being taken there, too," she added quickly.

"Take her to Ella Vee's," Garrett said abruptly.

Rylan nodded at his brother's suggestion, and at her questioning look explained, "Ella Vee is a good friend of the family. She's widowed, owns a large, two-story house, and rents out the rooms on the upper level."

The first ray of optimism blossomed within Jenna. "That'll be perfect."

Rylan's lips twisted with wry amusement. "Okay, Ella Vee's it is. I'll be out front when you're ready to go."

He left the house, and strained silence reigned once more.

Jenna was the first to shatter the quiet. "I guess I'll go gather up my things from your room and be on my way with Rylan."

Stepping closer to her host, she extended her hand in a very business-like manner. "Thank you again, Garrett, for everything."

He hesitated a brief moment, then slipped his hand into hers, throwing her attempt at impersonal right out the window. She shivered, startled by the warmth of his sliding palm and the graze of his calloused fingers against her soft skin. But it was his dark eyes as they merged with hers that caused her heart to beat just a bit faster.

He pulled his hand back, hastily severing the connection, as if fearing where that simple touch might

lead...*again.* "Try and stay out of trouble, Jenna."
His voice was low and rough.

She struggled to regain her composure. "I'll do
my best, but lately, trouble seems to find *me.*"

CHAPTER FOUR

THE woman was trouble with a capital "T."

Three days later, Garrett still found himself thinking about Jenna Phillips and those generous curves of hers, that luxurious curly hair he found too fascinating, and those soft periwinkle eyes that had the ability to turn him inside out with restless wanting.

Trouble, trouble, trouble.

With a grunt that clearly expressed his moodiness, he hit the buttons on the calculator on his desk and jotted down the numbers on the electrical estimate in front of him. He'd managed to avoid running into Jenna in town, but that didn't stop her from slipping into his dreams at night and haunting his waking hours during the day. It didn't help that the shirt he'd worn today—the shirt she'd slept in, and the same one his daughter had so helpfully hung in his closet when she'd picked up his room after Jenna had left their house Sunday morning—held her subtle feminine scent. Every breath he took made him ache for something he had no business desiring.

Yeah, she was trouble, all right. The kind that had his libido in knots. The kind he couldn't shake no matter how hard he tried.

Lisa and Rylan's voices drifting from the outer offices of Blackwell Engineering redirected Garrett's thoughts back to the present. He welcomed the diversion. His brother was on his way to a new project in the city and needed a set of blueprints for the job. The plans were still spread out on the drafting table in the back room where Garrett had been reviewing them earlier, and needed to be rolled and tubed.

Setting aside the estimate paperwork, he pushed away from his desk and headed out to the receptionist area. Rylan had retreated to his own office, and Lisa sat behind her desk, sifting through a pile of receivables as she fielded a sudden influx of incoming calls.

He frowned as he watched her handle each task efficiently, but there was no denying that she looked haggard and sounded fatigued. So far, the ad in the paper had only brought in three potential women to interview, and none had been to Lisa's liking. Considering his sister had commandeered the secretarial duties for Blackwell Engineering since the age of eighteen, he supposed it was difficult for her to hand over the reins to a stranger. Sooner or later, she'd have no choice...and Garrett was opting toward *sooner*.

Garrett was in the process of rolling up the designs Rylan needed when his brother sauntered into the drafting room in his normal laid-back manner. While Garrett had become the responsible, reliable son after their father's death in order to take over the family business and help make ends meet, Rylan had managed to maintain his easygoing attitude about women, work, and life in general. Though he was dependable and a hard worker, Rylan took very little seriously, and nothing seemed to bother him.

"Hey, bro, guess who I saw last night at Leisure Pointe?"

The mischievous grin tugging the corner of

Rylan's mouth and the anticipation in his voice was enough to pique a mild bout of curiosity from Garrett. "I have no idea," he replied, securing a rubber band around the plans before slipping them into a sturdy tube and capping off the end. "Who did you see?"

Folding his arms over his chest, Rylan rocked back on the heels of his work boots, looking too smug for Garrett's liking. "*Your* Jenna Phillips was there."

Garrett's stomach tightened at the mere mention of Jenna's name. She hardly seemed the type to spend a weeknight evening in a *bar* of all places, but he had to admit that he didn't know Jenna all that well. Certainly not well enough to know what she did in her leisure time.

Handing the blueprints over to Rylan, he released a taut stream of breath. "Jenna isn't *mine*," he clarified for his brother's benefit as nonchalantly as possible.

Rylan tapped the tube against Garrett's broad shoulder and waggled his brows wolfishly. "I'm sure she could be, if you played your cards right."

A surge of annoyance gripped Garrett, and he struggled for indifference. "Unlike you, Ry, I don't need a woman in my life."

Rylan scoffed at that statement, his gaze perceptive despite his carefree disposition. "Well, maybe if you did have a woman in your life, you wouldn't be as uptight as you've been the last couple of days."

Garrett wished he could take offense at his brother's comment, but the sad fact was, Rylan *was* right about his cantankerous temperament. And it was all Jenna's fault—and his own for allowing her to get under his skin.

Determined to put the woman from his mind, he went back to his office, sat behind his desk, and resumed working on his estimate.

Rylan showed up in his doorway seconds later and entered the room without an invitation. "Aren't you the least bit curious to know what she was doing at Leisure Pointe?"

"Not really," he lied, unable to look Rylan in the eye. Keeping his head lowered, he penciled in a dimension, calculated the price, and summed up the total.

Rylan took one of the seats in front of Garrett's desk. "She's working there as a waitress."

A jolting shock went through Garrett, and his gaze jerked to Rylan. He was positive he'd heard his brother incorrectly, because as difficult as it was to envision Jenna having a casual drink at Leisure Pointe, it was even more impossible to imagine her *working* there serving drinks.

He shook his head. Hard. "She's doing *what*?"

"She's Harlan's new waitress."

This time, Garrett heard him perfectly.

"But I thought you said you weren't interested," Rylan added quickly. With a triumphant smirk for riling Garrett, he stood and headed toward the door.

"I'm not," he snapped after him, instantly regretting his tone that revealed *way* too much. Jaw clenched, he forced himself to ignore Rylan's exit.

Halfway across the room, his brother stopped and turned back around. "I have to say, Jenna looks damn good in tight jeans and a formfitting T-shirt," he said of the practical, but enticing uniforms the waitresses wore.

Garrett tossed his pencil onto the blotter and lifted his head, scowling darkly at Rylan. His look said what he didn't put into words—*what were you doing ogling Jenna?*

Rylan held up his free hand to ward off Garrett's wrath. "Hey, I wasn't the only one who noticed what an incredible body she has."

And he'd felt those soft, luscious curves pressed against him the night he'd rescued her, knew just how responsive her body was to his touch. The thought of another man attempting to get that close to her started a slow, possessive heat in his veins that didn't bode well for him.

He didn't care what Jenna did, he told himself firmly.

"You can tell she's never served drinks before," Rylan went on thoughtfully. "I mean, she's learning quick, but she's so out of place in the rowdy bar. And unlike Becky, she doesn't know how to handle the advances some of the guys have made toward her."

"Who's making advances?" Garrett asked before he could stop the flow of words.

Rylan shrugged as if it didn't matter, but there was enough amusement dancing in his eyes to let Garrett know his brother was deliberately taunting him.

"Out with it, Ry," he said, his voice rumbling in his throat like a deep growl. "Who?"

"Beau is the biggest culprit," he admitted, his frown reflecting his own displeasure of the situation. "He thinks it's amusing to take advantage of how polite and seemingly innocent she is. Harlan told Beau and his cohorts last night to keep their hands and come-ons to themselves, but Beau in particular has a hard time listening to anyone."

Every muscle in Garrett's body went rigid at the mention of Beau, and it took an excruciating effort to remind himself that he wasn't Jenna's bodyguard. "So, what do you expect me to do about it?"

"Nothing, I guess. I just thought you'd like to know what Jenna is doing." Rylan met his gaze, his features drawn into an uncharacteristically somber expression. "Garrett, she doesn't belong working at Leisure Pointe. You know that as much as I do."

She's not my responsibility. He chanted that litany over and over in his mind. "Jenna is a big girl, and she's not my problem to worry about." Hadn't she basically told him that same thing Sunday before she'd left his house? "She's her own person, and is free to do as she pleases."

"Yeah, I guess you're right," Rylan conceded with a sigh. "I thought I'd keep an eye on her tonight, just in case Beau decides to harass her, but I've got a date with Emma and we won't be going to Leisure Pointe. So, I guess Jenna is on her own."

Garrett picked up his pencil again and reached for a file folder on his desk, refusing to rise to the bait his brother dangled in front of him. "Yep, guess so."

Damn Rylan anyway, Garrett thought irritably. His brother had known exactly what he was doing that morning at the office when he'd told him about Jenna's new job, and Beau's harassment. Obviously,

Rylan thought Jenna needed a protector, and believed Garrett was the man for the job.

Maybe Garrett wouldn't mind the assignment so much if he hadn't been burned in the past by his wife. He knew firsthand that entangling himself in another woman's problems wouldn't be good for the quiet, stable lifestyle he'd created for himself and Chelsea. Nor was Jenna conducive to his emotional, and physical, well-being.

Turning his truck into Leisure Pointe's full parking lot, he pulled into the empty slot another car was vacating. The popular nightspot was as busy as it had been Saturday night. And just like then, Garrett knew he'd spend the evening trying to protect Jenna's virtue from the more unsavory patrons who frequented the establishment.

Cursing his brother's interference once again, and grumbling at his own weakness for letting this woman get to him, he exited his vehicle and crossed the graveled parking lot toward the entrance of Leisure Pointe.

He'd vowed this morning that he wouldn't get involved with Jenna and the hazards of her choice of occupation. Swore he didn't care about her predicament, and sternly reminded himself that he wasn't duty-bound to be her guardian.

Yet all day long he'd thought of nothing but Jenna, and by afternoon, guilt plagued him. Despite not wanting to be responsible for this complex, runaway bride, he knew if something happened to Jenna that he might have been able to prevent, he'd never forgive himself for ignoring Rylan's subtle prompting, and his own male instincts.

Once Rylan left for his date with Emma for the

evening, Garrett had spurred into immediate action. After calling Lisa to make arrangements for her to watch Chelsea for a few hours, he'd dropped his daughter off, then headed to Leisure Pointe.

Now that he was here, he again questioned his sanity, which seemed to have taken a leave of absence lately.

Stepping inside the bar, he cast a quick, sweeping glance around the place, and immediately honed in on a familiar, curvaceous backside displayed in snug denim as Jenna sashayed toward a booth with a tray of drinks. His other clue to her identity was the wild spiral curls she attempted to restrain with a clip at the nape of her neck. The luxurious strands were as uniquely Jenna's as that enticing beauty mark above her upper lip.

Arriving at the table, she bent over to serve the couple sitting there, and his blood pressure spiked. And just as Rylan had indicated, half of the male population in the room were also appreciating Jenna's head-turning figure. The woman was so naturally sensual, in looks and mannerisms. Yet she seemed completely oblivious to her allure, and the stares cast her way.

Shaking off the possessive spark infusing his blood, he looked for a place to sit. Finding a small table in a corner of the bar where he could make himself inconspicuous, he made his way through the lively crowd and seated himself for a long night of surveillance.

While he waited for either Becky or Jenna to come and take his order, he scanned the patrons. His gaze narrowed when he caught sight of Beau Harding sitting with a group of young men. The other man was loud, obnoxious, and even from a distance Garrett could hear crude comments spilling from his mouth.

"My goodness, I'd hate to be the person on the receiving end of that dark look of yours."

Startled out of his brooding thoughts by a soft, feminine voice, he glanced up and found Jenna standing next to him, a small round tray in hand, and a friendly smile in place.

He didn't waste time with polite talk. "Jenna, what are you doing here?"

"I'm working," she replied easily, unperturbed by the abrupt tone of his voice. Retrieving a pad of paper and pen from the pocket of the apron tied around her waist, she glanced back at him, ready to take his order. "So, what can I get for you?"

"A beer," he said automatically, and followed that up with, "Why *here?*"

She jotted down his preference on the notepad. "Because Harlan needed an extra waitress, I needed a job, and the money is decent." She shifted the tray to her other hand and set a napkin on the table in front of him. "And if you need more personal reasons, I have rent that's due to Ella Vee, I'm looking to purchase a used vehicle which I need to get around in so I don't have to walk to and from work, and I still have outstanding bills to pay. Quite simply put, employment equals a paycheck."

Her answer was logical and legitimate, her fortitude equally unwavering. For as much as Garrett knew he should get up, walk out, and leave Jenna to do as she pleased, that damnable, innate sense of obligation kept him firmly in his seat. "You don't belong working here, in a *bar* of all places."

A delicately arched brow lifted mockingly. "According to you, I don't belong in this town, period. Why should my working here, or anywhere in Danby, be any different?"

He sighed, unable to refute that he had given her that impression. "You know what I mean, Jenna." And if she didn't understand where he was coming from, he'd explain it to her so she did. "This rowdy bar is no place for a lady like you—working, or otherwise."

Her congenial smile remained in place, but a sudden resignation shadowed her gaze. "Garrett, sometimes we have to do things that we don't necessarily want to, just to make ends meet. This isn't the first time I've done something because I had no other viable alternative. And since I have no desire to return to the city, and my choices are limited, I'm making the best of what's offered."

His lips pursed. "Jenna—"

"I appreciate your concern," she said, cutting him off before he could issue another objection. "But I'm extremely busy right now and I don't have time to argue with you. I have orders to put in, and drinks to deliver."

She turned and headed back to the bar, and he let her go, frustrated beyond all reason at her curt brush-off. Confusing emotions twisted within him, and his annoyance increased when Becky delivered his drink instead of Jenna, and the other woman told him she'd be taking any further orders.

So, he sat there for the next two hours, nursing his one beer and alternating between watching Jenna who steadfastly avoided him, and monitoring Beau, who continued ordering more rounds of drinks for him and his friends. And the more liquor Beau consumed, the more loose-tongued and verbally offensive he became. Even a warning from Harlan didn't soften or waylay the other man's comments and overt flirting tactics with the female patrons and waitresses.

Then Beau made the mistake of touching Jenna after she'd delivered their beers—a deliberate, presumptuous pass of his hand over her bottom. His advance was disturbing and personal enough to make Jenna politely ask Beau to please stop, which the other man took as a challenge.

Grabbing her arm and knocking the tray from her hand, Beau pulled her down onto his lap. Jenna's eyes widened in shock as she found herself draped across the other man's thighs. Beau and his friends laughed raucously at his bold move.

Garrett's temper exploded in a hot, red haze. Without giving a thought to his actions, or the kind of speculation he might stir for defending Jenna, he bolted from his seat and strode purposefully across the crowded room. Out of the corner of his eye he saw Harlan rounding the bar to handle the situation himself, but Garrett didn't give the owner the chance.

By the time Garrett arrived at Beau's table, Jenna was standing again, but thoroughly humiliated by what had happened. Her face was red with embarrassment, and the mortification touching her features made Garrett all the more furious at Harding.

In a move meant to protect Jenna, he stepped in front of her to confront Beau, who glanced up at him with an insolent look. Garrett wasn't the least bit intimidated by the other man.

"Touch the lady again, and you'll find yourself arrested for sexual harassment." His voice vibrated with unmistakable warning.

"Yeah?" Beau attempted to stand, and swaggered slightly before catching his balance. Then he puffed out his chest belligerently. "You and what army are going to stop me, Blackwell?"

Garrett's hands clenched into tight fists at his sides. He despised men who preyed on women's vulnerabilities, and Beau was as sleazy as they came. He didn't even want to think about what else Beau might have tried with Jenna if he hadn't been around to intercept the other man's advances.

"Trust me, Harding," he said in a low, dangerous tone any smart man would heed. "The only person you have to worry about is *me*."

Beau's lip curled in a sneer. "Who's gonna stand up for *her* when you're not around?"

Furious at the other man's insinuation and the subtle threat to Jenna, Garrett stepped toward Beau, intending to shove him up against the wall and rattle his arrogant facade. But before Garrett could fully execute the move, Harlan reached the table and planted himself between the two men.

"Settle down, boys," the bartender said sternly.

Garrett immediately backed off, disgusted with himself for nearly starting a barroom brawl in Harlan's establishment.

Harlan motioned to Becky, who'd been watching the heated encounter with as much fascination and interest as the rest of the patrons. "Bring Beau and everyone at his table a round of strong, hot coffee," he ordered, then gave Harding a pointed look. "Then I suggest you and your friends leave peacefully, or I can call the sheriff to escort you out. The choice is yours.''

Though Beau sat back down without argument to wait the arrival of his coffee to counter all the liquor he'd consumed, he shot Garrett a dark, hostile look that said he'd only been temporarily subdued.

Dammit all, Garrett thought, narrowing his gaze on the other man in an equally aggressive stare. Judging by the cocksure gleam in Beau's eyes, Garrett knew without a doubt that Jenna would continue to be the center of Beau's salacious advances for as long as she worked at Leisure Pointe. Garrett was forced to admit that Rylan was right—Jenna was way out of her element and easy prey for Beau and his cohorts, or any other man who decided to take advantage of her inexperience as a bar waitress.

Harlan gave a satisfied nod that all was back under control, and turned to Jenna, who still hadn't completely recovered her shaken composure. ''Jenna, you can deliver the drinks I left at the bar to the corner table.''

Her gaze skirted away from Beau, and she inhaled a deep breath to regain her equilibrium and poise. ''Okay.''

Seeing past all that outward strength to the hint of insecurity and uncertainties beneath caused something fierce and unexplainable to well within Garrett at that moment—an emotion he refused to examine too closely for fear of what it implied. Neither did he want to take the time to analyze the decision he was about to make on Jenna's behalf.

She bent and picked up the tray she'd dropped during Beau's assault, but before she could do Harlan's bidding, Garrett grabbed her wrist, stopping her retreat. Her pulse leapt beneath the light press of his fingers, and she met his gaze with a startled frown.

Taking the tray from her unsteady fingers, he pressed it into Harlan's hand. "You're gonna have to find yourself another waitress," he told the older man succinctly. "Jenna's quitting."

She gasped, the wordless sound filled with outrage. Before she could gain her breath to refute him, he promptly dragged her out of the bar at a clipped pace she could barely keep up with, and into the cool summer night.

Garrett hustled his way through the parking lot toward his truck, with Jenna still in tow. The area was well-lit, but deserted, except for the constant chirp of crickets and night insects.

Just as they reached his vehicle, she unexpectedly dug in her heels, and her sneakered feet skidded along the gravel lot, jarring them both to a stop. She pulled her arm back, finagling her way out of his hold, and unleashed the fury he saw leaping to life in her bright eyes.

"What do you think you're doing?" she asked, bristling with indignation.

"That should be obvious," he chided recklessly. "I'm saving you from yourself."

She stared at him incredulously. "I don't remember *asking* to be saved or rescued, by you or anyone else." Breasts heaving, she advanced toward him, and jabbed a finger against his chest to express the extent of her anger. "Your stunt back there in the bar was barbaric and antiquated, and I don't appreciate you making decisions for me that I'm capable of making for myself, *or* your take-charge attitude."

His entire body grew rigid with sudden awareness. She stood too close. Heated tension arched between them. The fiery sensation twisted through his
belly, and sparked a flare of desire he struggled to
suppress.

The word, *trouble, trouble, trouble,* echoed in his
mind.

"The way I saw things, my interference was *necessary.*" Jamming his hands on his hips, he lowered
his face closer to hers, but she didn't back away as
he'd hoped. No, she stubbornly held her ground. "I
can't be here every night to make sure Beau or some
other drunk doesn't harass you."

"Did I ask you to?" She didn't wait for his response, since they both knew the answer to her question. "I thought we'd established that I'm not your
responsibility."

"I watched you tonight for *two hours,* Jenna,
dodging advances and come-ons while trying to
keep up with drink orders from the rowdy crowd.
You're so out of place working in that bar, and
everyone knows it but *you.*" He shoved his fingers
through his hair, but the action did nothing to ease
the multitude of emotions tumbling through him.
"Granted, I might have overreacted, but I don't regret pulling you out of there. I did it for your own
good."

And his own peace of mind.

"How do you know what's good for me?" she
demanded, tossing her head back defiantly. Moon-
light illuminated her beautiful features and intensi-
fied the opposition glittering in her eyes. "Dammit,
Garrett, how do you know what I *want or need?*"

The challenge in her tone taunted him, and the only thing that filtered through his mind in that moment was what he *wanted,* what he *needed,* and what he'd denied himself since the night he'd first met her. Wrapping an arm around her waist, he pulled her flush against him, and used his other hand to cup her cheek and tip her face up toward his.

Their gazes clashed. Her hands were trapped against his chest, and she looked startled, but not at all frightened. In fact, with every labored breath they shared, rebellion glowed in the depth of her eyes, a silent dare that provoked every one of his baser male impulses...*to conquer, claim and possess.*

He ached to taste her, and before he changed his mind or she realized what he intended, he dropped his mouth over hers. Her breath caught on a moan, but she didn't resist or protest. Soft lips molded to his, and he savored the warm texture, the lush feel, then slid his hand around to the nape of her neck and pressed his mouth more firmly to hers. She grew pliant and opened for him, allowing him to explore deeper, forbidden territory.

His tongue glided along hers, hot and urgent. While their first kiss had been one of comfort and gratitude, this one was exciting, sensual, and oh, so satisfying. Her mouth was giving and sweet, pure magic, and he couldn't seem to get enough of her. Heart pounding heavily in his chest, he embraced the rich, insatiable sensations she evoked, and sank deeper still.

Their bodies brushed enticingly. He felt the budded tips of her breasts, the friction of her denim-clad thighs rubbing across his, and every caress, every subtle nuance, all worked together to inflame him even more. The *wanting* and *need* grew to startling proportions, flowing hot and molten through his veins, like a volatile, potent mix of fire and kerosene.

Trouble, trouble, trouble.

The sound of conversation and laughter from people exiting Leisure Pointe provided a much needed dose of reality and brought Garrett to his senses. With a low groan, he pulled his mouth from hers and staggered back a step, stunned by the depth of his response to her.

She stared up at him and touched her glistening lips, looking just as dazed, all her previous anger having dissipated in his embrace. And it struck Garrett that he had no idea what this woman *wanted,* or *needed,* and he was beginning to suspect that nobody had ever taken the time or care to discover what Jenna Phillips longed for or desired.

He was just as guilty. He hadn't asked her permission for that kiss. No, he'd *taken* of his own volition, and while she hadn't issued any objection, he'd had no right to be so brazen in his approach, not when he had no idea if Jenna still harbored feelings for her ex-fiancé.

Feeling way too philosophical over the situation, he gently grasped her arm and ushered her to the passenger side of his vehicle. Opening the door, he motioned her inside the lighted interior. "Get in the truck, Jenna, and I'll take you back to Ella Vee's."

She complied without argument, which was enough to tell Garrett that his kiss had thrown her for a loop and she was still recovering from the experience. Shutting the door after her, he walked around the front of the truck to the driver's side. He inhaled a deep breath to clear his head and the arousal buzzing through his body, but there was little he could do to dispel the feminine scent that swirled around him, or the honeyed taste of her lingering on his lips.

He released a low, tortured groan, knowing he was in for another long, restless night.

CHAPTER FIVE

SHE never should have let him kiss her, Jenna thought as Garrett drove toward the boarding house in silence. A chaste, comforting brush of lips was one thing, but no way had she been prepared for Garrett's brand of sensuality and potent masculinity that came with his deep, all-consuming kiss. And never would she dream that her own response would be so uninhibited.

After years of suppressing feminine needs beneath a layer of sophistication and decorum for the sake of propriety, she finally knew what the heat of passion felt like, and just how sweet desire could taste. She'd enjoyed every bit of Garrett's seduction, and had wanted more. That particular revelation was shocking, thrilling, and most of all frightening to her emotional stability because it went against every piece of advice her mother had ever given her.

She closed her eyes, remembering those frequent lectures with too much clarity. Her mother had spent her life searching for a man who'd take care of her, but her choices hadn't been the best, and she'd always ended up used, hurt, and alone. When Jenna had turned fifteen and boys started noticing her blossoming figure, her mother had taken her own experiences with men and used them as examples of what she didn't want for her daughter.

Jodie had never been lucky in love, and drilled into Jenna the importance of respectability and making practical decisions when it came to the opposite sex. Love and frivolous emotions would only bring her heartache, her mother had assured her, but no one could strip her of her virtue and dignity. No, Jenna had managed to do that for herself when she'd accepted a less than reputable job to earn extra money to pay off her mother's medical bills.

That particular offense had caught up to her at the altar on her wedding day, and sent Sheldon and his family into a furor of shock and disbelief. Then came the disgrace and humiliation of her actions, and the knowledge that not only was she not good enough for Sheldon, but her past had the ability to destroy his reputation, and possibly his career.

She shuddered at the awful memory, knowing her past decision would have repercussions that would forever impair her chances of grasping the kind of happiness she craved for herself, especially finding a man who respected her enough to offer her marriage. It was all she ever wanted, but the fear of another scandal would always be a threat, and what man would want a wife who harbored such a shocking secret?

Certainly not an honorable, *respectable* man like Garrett.

Cheeks burning with the provocative memory of just how eager she'd been with him in the parking lot, she blinked her lashes open and gazed out the window to the darkness of night. She knew she ought to be ashamed of her unabashed behavior, but truth be told, she'd craved Garrett's kiss. Never once had it crossed her mind to issue a protest or refuse him, and she harbored no regrets for allowing him the liberties she had.

Shameless of her, she admitted, but she'd been drawn to the intensity she'd seen flickering in his eyes and the hunger that had been directed solely at her. She'd never been the recipient of such overwhelming sensuality—not even with Sheldon, who'd never inspired anything more than affection. And even though Garrett's kiss had been instigated in a fit of temper, there was no denying the currents of excitement that had rippled between them, or the gentleness of his touch. A shiver of remembered pleasure coursed through her before she could stop the heady sensation.

"Are you okay?"

Garrett's deep voice shattered the silence. She pulled herself out of her thoughts, and realized they were parked at the curb in front of Ella Vee's two-story house, with the engine idling.

She glanced his way, his serious features illuminated by the streetlamp beside the truck. He was back to gruff and distant, and the switch from breathtakingly sensual man to brusque attitude frustrated her. Especially after what had just transpired between them.

"It's nice of you to ask, considering I'm unemployed because of that stunt you pulled back at the bar," she said wryly. "I'm sure once everyone hears about tonight's fiasco, both of us are going to be dragged into the middle of some interesting gossip."

"Wouldn't be the first time I'm the topic of conversation around this town," he muttered beneath his breath.

She frowned, studying his profile and the grim set of his jaw. Curiosity urged her to ask, "What do you mean by that?"

His hands gripped the steering wheel and his eyes glowed with a bitterness she didn't fully understand. "My wife had a way of drawing attention to herself, and I was always smack dab in the center of the speculation."

He didn't offer any more than that tidbit of information, but it was obvious to Jenna that Garrett's marriage had been a turbulent one. She fought the compelling urge to ask what, exactly, had happened between him and his wife that had made him so wary and distrustful of women, especially *her*. But his answer made little difference to them, since that kiss had been a fluke and wouldn't be happening again.

"I'm not at fault for what happened at Leisure Pointe, Garrett," she said softly. "I didn't ask you to be my guardian. All I'm trying to do is fit in and earn a living, and you're making it difficult for me to do so."

He blew out a harsh stream of breath, releasing the tension that had bunched his shoulders. "I'll talk to Harlan about giving you your job back, if that's what you want."

Jenna bit the inside of her cheek at Garrett's dutiful suggestion. While she'd been initially furious with him for taking matters into his own hands, deep inside she was touched beyond reason that he'd been her champion. She'd never meant so much to anyone that they'd go to such lengths to protect her, to make her feel so safe.

If she was completely honest with herself, she'd have to admit that she wasn't suited to working in a bar. She'd known that from the first order she'd taken, but accepting the position had been a means to an end. She wasn't a stranger to taking whatever job necessary to pay bills, no matter how unsavory, but she'd like to be able to support herself without having to resort to less than ideal choices in employment. Something stable, secure, and dignified.

And there was also the fact that Harlan hadn't tried to stop Garrett, or her, from leaving his establishment. Which led her to believe the bartender agreed with Garrett's decision to end her employment at Leisure Pointe.

She opened the passenger door, shedding bright light in the small cab. His dark eyes watched her, waiting for an answer to his offer to talk to Harlan on her behalf...*if that's what she wanted.*

She shook her head. "All I want, all I've *ever* wanted, is to *belong.* I don't expect you to understand my simple dreams, Garrett, not when you come from a close, loving family, but I've never had that sense of acceptance, not even with Sheldon." And her biggest fear was that her past would keep her from grasping that kind of security and happiness for herself in the future. "Now I'm on my own, and I don't want to rely on anyone for anything if I don't have to. I'm trying to make an honest living and pick up the pieces of my life, and all I ask is that you let me do that here in Danby."

With that, she hopped out of the truck and headed toward the house, feeling Garrett's gaze every step of the way.

All I want is to belong.

Jenna's words echoed in Garrett's mind, weighed heavily on his conscience, and compounded the guilt that had been his constant companion since he'd dropped Jenna off at Ella Vee's three days ago. He glanced across the dinner table at Rylan as they ate Sunday dinner at Lisa's house. If it hadn't been for his brother's goading, he wouldn't be in this mess in the first place.

"Your bright idea to watch over Jenna certainly worked out well, Ry," he drawled, unable to keep the sarcastic bite from his tone.

Rylan grabbed a warm roll from the basket on the table and slathered butter on it, looking nonplussed. "I *never* said for you to quit Jenna's job for her."

"Jenna shouldn't be working in a place like Leisure Pointe, anyway," Lisa said, adding her own opinion to the matter.

Rylan sent his sister an agreeable grin. "That's exactly what I tried to tell Garrett. Not that he'd listen to *me*."

"I *did* listen to you," he argued as he pushed back Chelsea's glass of milk from the edge of the table so they didn't end up with an accident. "That's why Jenna is currently *unemployed*."

"Just imagine what could have happened if you *hadn't* been there the other night," Duane offered, reaching for a bowl of mashed potatoes.

The possible scenarios that filled Garrett's head weren't pleasant ones. He didn't trust Beau, and there was no telling how far the other man would have gone if Garrett hadn't been around to intercept his advances. But protecting Jenna's virtue was one thing, quitting her job on her behalf had been too presumptuous on his part—a decision made in the heat of the moment. One he'd come to regret with each passing day, just as much as that kiss they'd shared.

Worse than feeling awful for costing Jenna her job, Garrett was *responsible*. In a way that didn't bode well for his peaceful, solitary life. In a way that tied his stomach up in a dozen different knots because he just *knew* that burdensome emotion would cause him the kind of grief and turmoil he'd managed to avoid since Angela's death.

Lisa placed a hand on his arm and gave it a gentle squeeze. ''I know you're not happy about the outcome of all this, but you did the right thing, Garrett.''

And he *always* did the right thing.

His sister knew him too well. His whole family did. Ever since his father's death, he'd assumed the role of caretaker and head of the household, and protecting those he cared about had become a natural instinct. He'd just never guessed how far that ingrained habit would lead him…straight into Angela's tangled web of deceit. He'd learned with Angela that doing the right thing didn't necessarily pay off in the end.

He'd given, Angela had taken, and she'd repaid him by deceiving him in ways that had forever changed the trusting man he'd once been. Without a doubt, he was more cautious where women were concerned, including Jenna Phillips, who had a way of reaching past his defenses. There was something inherently guileless about her that made him want to believe she was exactly as she seemed—a woman who was searching for a place where she belonged.

But he still had no idea what had sent her bolting on her wedding day, and that mystery niggled at him, made him wonder what secrets she was hiding and running from.

"You know, there is a way to make up for all this."

"How?" Garrett asked, skeptical of the bright, eager look on Lisa's face.

Her smile blossomed into a full-fledged grin. "You still haven't hired someone to work the office in my absence—"

"No," he said, abruptly cutting her off. He knew exactly where she was heading with her suggestion, and he wanted no part in her scheme.

"But Jenna would be perfect. I remember you telling me that she was a secretary in St. Louis—"

"No."

She frowned at his stubborn attitude. "Why not?"

Three pairs of eyes stared at him, asking the same question, wanting the same answer.

Because the woman totally and completely wreaks havoc with my mind and body, he thought.

He dragged a hand along his taut jaw and settled for a version of the truth. "She's more of a distraction than I want or need."

Rylan's deep chuckle raked on Garrett's nerves. "Her kind of distraction is not a bad thing."

He glared at his brother, which Garrett knew he'd been doing an awful lot lately. Just another way how Jenna affected him, making him feel possessive when he'd never before been the jealous type. "Knock it off, Ry."

"Garrett, it's a great idea." Lisa caught her breath as one of the twins gave her a good swift kick in the belly, reminding him that his sister's due date was rapidly approaching. She caressed the bulging spot as if to soothe the babes within. "In fact, Jenna could work the same hours I do now, and watch

Chelsea in the afternoons after summer camp so Chelsea isn't stuck at the office with you.''

"I want Jenna to watch me," Chelsea piped in, just as eager as the rest of the trio at the dinner table. "Please, Daddy?"

Garrett rubbed at the sharp ache throbbing in his temple, feeling as though his control of the situation was rapidly slipping through his fingers. He was reluctant to agree to what his family thought was appropriate, when he was the better judge of what was best for *him*. And it wasn't Jenna Phillips.

Unfortunately, guilt and accountability were a powerful persuasion. He resented the protective feelings she evoked, disliked even more his attraction to her, but he'd never been one to shirk his responsibilities. Since he was culpable for Jenna losing her job at Leisure Pointe, the least he could do was offer her Lisa's job at the office, and with Chelsea in the afternoons, until his sister was able to return to work. It was a win-win situation all the way around, just so long as he didn't kiss her again.

Dropping his napkin on his plate, he pushed his half-eaten dinner away. "All right," he said, conceding to his family's wishes. "You all win. I'll stop by Ella Vee's on the way home and offer Jenna Lisa's job. But it's just a temporary arrangement, until Jenna finds something else, or Lisa returns from maternity leave."

"Perfect," his sister said, looking entirely too pleased with the situation.

"Daddy, look, there's Jenna!" Chelsea said, bouncing excitedly on the front passenger seat of his truck.

Garrett brought the vehicle to a stop at the curb

of Ella Vee's two-story house, his gaze following the direction of his daughter's pointing finger. Sure enough, Jenna was out front watering the flower beds flanking the house and porch, stopping occasionally to pull a weed or pluck a dead leaf from one of the planters, then tossing the foliage into a bucket. It was early evening, just after seven with about another hour of daylight, and much cooler than it had been that afternoon.

She wore sensible summer clothes he assumed she'd bought at the thrift store in town, and he had to admit that she filled out the second-hand outfit extremely well. A plain pink T-shirt tied beneath her full breasts to keep cool, and a pair of cut-off jean shorts displayed those long, slender legs that had starred in his nightly fantasies. Her feet were bare, and she looked...*incredible,* as fresh and appealing as the girl next door.

Removing the keys from the ignition, he shook off his fascination. Unfortunately, there wasn't much he could do for the need and desire she so effortlessly elicited. And despite every lecture he'd given himself about keeping his distance from this woman, there was something about her that roused instincts he knew could only lead to trouble. Keeping his emotions under lock and key was of utmost importance, especially since he'd be working with Jenna on a daily basis, *if* she even accepted his offer.

Waving wildly, Chelsea scrambled from the truck and dashed across the lawn, her blond ponytail bouncing on her shoulders. "Hi, Jenna!"

"Well, hello, Chelsea." Turning off her sprayer and setting the hose aside, Jenna bestowed a glorious smile upon his daughter that Garrett envied.

"What a wonderful surprise it is to see you." Her greeting was sincere, her pleasure at seeing Chelsea genuine.

Keeping a listening ear to their conversation, Garrett adopted a more leisurely pace than his daughter had as he headed up the walkway. The two of them interacted easily, assuring him that he could depend on Jenna to watch over his daughter, and be a friend to Chelsea as well.

"You're so lucky that you get to live here with Ms. Ella Vee." Chelsea sniffed at the air, seemingly catching a scent drifting on the slight breeze. "It smells like she's making peanut butter cookies. She makes the best ones in the whole wide world!"

"I do believe she is baking cookies," Jenna confirmed, then tapped Chelsea on the tip of her nose. "You've got yourself quite a sniffer."

Chelsea giggled and wrinkled her nose. "I'm gonna go see if I can help her!"

Chelsea disappeared into the house and Jenna glanced his way. She'd piled her thick mass of curls atop her head with a large, clawlike clip, but a few strands managed to escape and curl around her face and along her neck. Up close, he noticed her nose and cheeks were pink from working out in the sun, and her eyes shone with a sudden wariness that eclipsed the warmth she'd reserved for his daughter.

He couldn't blame her for being apprehensive of him, and his visit. Their last encounter had been anything but congenial.

Her breasts rose and fell as she took a deep breath before addressing him. "Hello, Garrett."

Her soft voice wrapped around him like a caress, touching him in places he wished were more immune to her. "Hello, Jenna," he replied, inclining his head in polite greeting.

"Are you here to visit Ella Vee?" She waved a hand toward the front door. "She's in the kitchen—"

"I'm not here to see Ella Vee." He propped a booted foot on the bottom porch step. "I'm here to see you."

"Me?" Undeniable surprise laced her voice. "After the way we parted Thursday evening, I can't imagine what you need to speak with me about, or what's left to say."

He cringed, unable to fault her for expressing skepticism, sounding cautious, or thinking the absolute worst of him. He'd given her no reason to believe that there could ever be anything amicable between them. And he wasn't here to establish a close-knit friendship, but to vindicate himself of that damnable obligation his brother and sister had heaped upon him.

"I..." The words caught, and he cleared his throat and tried again. "I owe you an apology for my part in you losing your job the other night. I never should have interfered, and should have let Harlan handle the incident." Oh, how he wish he had!

"Apology accepted," she murmured.

Relief pervaded his system. He was quickly learning that Jenna wasn't a woman who held grudges. She took what life delivered and tried to make the best of the situation. He appreciated that quality now more than ever, which kept him from groveling for her forgiveness.

"About you losing your job..."

"Don't worry about it," she said before he could finish. "I went for an interview at the bank Friday afternoon, and Zach Morris expressed interest in possibly hiring me on as his personal secretary. I'm hoping it works out, since that's the kind of job I'm used to doing."

Garrett almost choked on the breath he'd inhaled. Zach was the vice president of operations at the bank, and a nice guy, but he was a known womanizer around town. Interesting that he'd never needed a personal secretary until Jenna happened to apply for a job.

More interesting was the fact that Garrett hated the thought of Jenna working in such close proximity for the other man. "Actually, that's why I came by today, to offer you a job."

Her expression reflected her astonishment. "Doing what?"

He released a tight breath. "I need a temporary secretary at the office while Lisa is on maternity leave, as well as someone to watch over Chelsea in the afternoons until I get home from work."

She didn't jump on the offer, but approached it guardedly. "Why *me?*" She suddenly stiffened, and didn't give him a chance to answer her question. "If you're doing this because you feel responsible for what happened with my job at Leisure Pointe…"

She let the words trail off, but her meaning was clear. She didn't want to be a charity case, a burden, and he was beginning to understand just how deeply her pride ran. A part of him couldn't help but respect her for being an independent woman intent on relying on her own resources.

Hiring her because of the loss of her waitress job

was only part of the reason he was offering her a position at Blackwell Engineering. The gut-level feelings she stirred were too perplexing to decipher, so he didn't even try.

"You said you were a secretary in St. Louis, so you have the skills it takes to run an office once you learn the basics, right?"

"Yes," she said slowly, "But so do temporaries."

"I don't trust just anyone with my daughter." Having witnessed the caring between her and Chelsea only moments ago, he knew with certainty that Jenna *was* the best candidate for the job.

Their gazes met and held for a long moment, the gold rimming her eyes breathtaking in its intensity and beauty. He felt light-headed, aroused, and annoyed with his response to her.

She crossed her arms over her chest and shook her head. "Garrett, I don't think working together would be a good idea."

The doubt he heard in her voice spurred him to desperate measures. "I'll double the salary Zach was willing to offer you."

She sucked in an audible breath, then quickly recovered from her shock. "Why should I give up something that might turn out to be permanent for a job that's only temporary?"

"Because I need you more than Zach does." He didn't mean to sound so possessive, but it seemed he had little control over those emotions where this woman was concerned.

She lifted a brow at his reasoning, a faint smile tipping the corner of her mouth with the beauty mark. "Garrett, I doubt you need *anyone*."

Her statement rang with too much truth. He'd always been so busy taking care of everyone else, from his family, to Angela, to Chelsea, that he'd never allowed himself to need or depend on anyone.

"Chelsea needs you," he amended. "And she adores you. I was going to try and juggle work and watching her at the office, but Lisa is right. Chelsea doesn't belong there, and you can give her the attention she needs until I get home in the evenings."

He watched her waver in her decision. Without thinking of the consequences that came with touching her, he slipped his fingers over the back of the hand she'd placed on the porch stair railing. Her gaze leapt to his, and his blood quickened with instantaneous awareness.

He struggled to ignore the heat shimmering between them. "I think we'd be doing each other a big favor that we'd both benefit from if you accepted my offer," he said in one last attempt to sway her.

The tip of her tongue flicked across her bottom lip, and she drew back her hand, severing the connection. "Are you willing to take the chance that people might talk about us?" Insecurities laced her voice, along with a subtle warning.

For as much as he didn't care for the speculation running rampant about him and Jenna because of his interference at Leisure Pointe last week, he realized he wanted to give her a chance—to fit in and belong, and gain the respectability she'd mentioned that first night he'd rescued her.

He owed her that much, and wanted desperately to be free of his personal debt to her. This offer was a start.

"We're already the talk around town, Jenna," he

stated with a shrug. "This is nothing more than a business proposition between you and I." And he planned to keep their relationship purely professional, too.

"You make it all sound so simple," she said, still sounding indecisive.

"There's no reason why it can't be simple, and beneficial to the both of us. You need a job, and I need a secretary, and a sitter for Chelsea."

"All right," she said softly. "I'll accept the job."

"Great." The one word escaped him on a rush of breath he hadn't realized he'd been holding until that moment. "You can start tomorrow morning. Lisa will be there to show you the basic procedures."

And all he had to do was keep direct interaction with Jenna to a minimum, and avoid being alone with her. Unfortunately, he had a feeling those rules were much easier said, than done.

CHAPTER SIX

FOR the first time since her wedding day, Jenna felt as though she was back in her element. Working for Garrett, doing all the things she was familiar with and had enjoyed in her position as a secretary back in St. Louis gave her a sense of rightness and dignity that made her outlook on the future much brighter than it had been a week ago. There was something to be said about being true to one's self and doing what felt *right*, rather than leading a life dictated by the kind of rules and expectations her mother had enforced since she was a young girl.

She shook her head in wonder at her personal revelation as she filed away one of the payables she'd recorded into the accounts ledger with Lisa's earlier help. "What in the world made me think I could be a stay-at-home wife and be happy?" she murmured to herself, unable to imagine spending her days planning dinner parties, and indulging in social luncheons.

"Did you say something?" a deep voice inquired.

Startled out of her musings, Jenna glanced over her shoulder as Garrett placed a sheaf of papers in the wire basket on her desk, looking too appealing in a short-sleeved knit shirt and formfitting jeans. She, on the other hand, had opted for a pair of slacks, sandals, and one of the silk shirts she'd packed for her honeymoon. Lisa had informed her that every day was "casual day" at Blackwell

Engineering, and to come to work wearing something comfortable. Jenna planned to take advantage of Lisa's suggestion.

After spending the morning training Jenna to run the front office, Lisa had gone home a few hours ago. While Garrett had been around the entire day, he'd made himself scarce. For the most part, he'd sequestered himself in his office and kept contact with her to a minimum.

She was mildly surprised that he'd struck up any kind of conversation now, but decided if they were going to spend so much time together the next few months it was best if they established a congenial working relationship. "I was just thinking out loud about how exhilarating it feels to do something that stimulates my mind more than delivering drinks." A satisfied smile touched her mouth. "I've missed this kind of work more than I'd realized."

He glanced briefly her way as he slipped a document into the fax, punched out a number, and hit the send button. "Lisa told me that you're catching on quick."

"It helps when you're at ease with office procedures and like what you're doing." She tucked a bill away for drafting supplies, then closed the filing cabinet drawer. She headed back to her desk, very aware of his warm gaze tracking her progress across the room. "This is a fascinating business. What made you decide to become an electrical engineer?"

His mouth pursed slightly, indicating his reluctance to talk about personal issues when it was so obvious to her that he wanted to keep things between them business-like.

"I'm not asking for trade secrets, Garrett," she

said, injecting humor into her tone. "I'm just wondering how Blackwell Engineering came about."

He rolled his shoulders, and his body relaxed a fraction. "My father was an electrician, and mainly catered to the residents of Danby. As soon as Rylan and I were old enough to learn the trade, we followed in Dad's footsteps."

"And?" she prompted, knowing there was more to his story.

A smile twitched the corner of his mouth at her persistence, but instead of brushing off her interest, he leaned his hip against the cabinet holding the fax machine and continued. "The company has always been family owned and operated, and when my dad died, Rylan and I inherited the business. We continued the miscellaneous electrical jobs in town while I went to college for a degree in electrical engineering. Once I graduated, Ry and I made the decision to expand the business and specialize in electrical contracting. Since we've started bidding on big projects near St. Louis, and being awarded those jobs, the company has grown beyond our expectations."

The pride in his voice was unmistakable. He was the kind of man who worked hard, and took nothing for granted. "How come you spend your days in the office instead of supervising those big jobs in the city?"

The fax machine spit out the document he'd sent, and Garrett carried it over to her desk, adding it to the pile in her basket. "Rylan prefers the field work and direct supervision, and I took over in the office to handle estimates, bidding, and contracts because that keeps me close to home for Chelsea."

Of course his daughter would be his main priority. Sighing wistfully, she brushed a wayward curl behind her ear, and his eyes followed the movement of her fingers, and lingered on the wild, disheveled mess that was her hair. The masculine hand resting at his side flexed into a fist, as if he had to physically restrain himself to keep from reaching out and touching her.

The notion made her heart skip a beat. "Where is your mother?" she asked, drawing his attention back to her face.

He exhaled a slow breath, seemingly grateful for the distracting question. "She moved to Iowa four years ago to live with her sister. We see her once or twice a year and I send Chelsea to visit her, too."

An unexpected swell of melancholy filled Jenna, and she spoke her thoughts without thinking. "Your daughter is very lucky to have so many people in her life who love her, especially since she lost her mother at such an early age."

He stared at her for a long moment, something fiercely protective swirling to life in the depths of his velvet-blue eyes. "Angela's death didn't affect Chelsea much, considering she wasn't around enough to form any kind of maternal bond with her. Angela's main priority was satisfying her own selfish wants and desires, and she gave little thought to how her actions might affect her baby daughter, or even the man she'd married."

The chill in his voice, the resentment etching his expression, caused a shiver to ripple down Jenna's spine. Judging by how self-centered Angela had been, was it no wonder Garrett didn't trust women easily? She detected deeper, more painful layers to his superficial account of his wife's behavior. She couldn't help wonder what had happened between the two of them, but she wasn't about to tap into that volatile mix of emotions.

He glanced at his watch, and smoothly changed the subject. "It's almost two. Why don't you quit here for the day and go on and pick up Chelsea from summer camp?" He retrieved a set of keys from a rack on the wall behind her desk. "Here's the keys to the extra company truck until you can afford to get yourself a vehicle." He pressed them into her hand.

Her stomach fluttered at his touch, a pleasant tickle that gradually invaded her entire system and reminded her of the soft, lush feel of his lips on hers. "Thank you. I'll see you at the house in a bit, then?" She gathered up her things to leave.

He shook his head. "I'm working late tonight on an estimate for a bid tomorrow." Averting his gaze, he absently rubbed at the back of his neck. "Rylan will probably be home before I am, and he'll watch Chelsea until I get there."

Recognizing his excuse for the diversion tactic it was, and understanding his reasons, she didn't push the issue.

He'd managed to finagle his way out of coming home to Jenna yesterday, and dealing with her presence in his *house*, but today Garrett wasn't so fortunate. Rylan caught on to his ploy to avoid Jenna and informed him that he wouldn't be his scapegoat every night of the week.

Easing out a tight breath between his teeth, Garrett climbed the porch steps to the front door. It was bad enough that he spent the day with Jenna at the office, overwhelmingly aware of every move she made and the light, floral scent that drifted from her riot of soft, curly hair when she happened to pass him. She entered his office often to ask questions after Lisa left, and engaged him in casual conversation whenever possible. She was prompt and efficient in getting her work done, and every bit of the distraction he'd feared.

He stepped inside the house and inhaled a fragrant, indolent scent of something rich and spicy. The delicious smell invading his senses made his mouth water and reminded his stomach that he'd skipped lunch. Reminded him, too, how he'd arrived home last night to a meat-and-potato casserole Jenna had made and left for him and the family to eat for supper. The hearty meal had been a satisfying, filling treat compared with the quick suppers he normally threw together in the evenings.

He followed the scent through the living room to the kitchen, and stopped short when he found Jenna standing at the stove, stirring a thick, aromatic substance bubbling in a big pot. The second thing he noticed was that she'd changed from her office attire into a black, one-piece swimsuit that enhanced her generous breasts and curves, and a wrap-around short skirt that displayed her long, slender legs all the way down to her bare feet. Her toenails were painted a pale shade of pink.

Her back was to him, and with her singing along to a pop rock tune playing on the radio on the counter, she obviously hadn't heard him arrive. Unable to help himself, he watched the sway of her hips, too fascinated by her uninhibited shimmies and the rhythmic movements of her body. She was utterly sensual, completely feminine, and she stirred everything from his emotions to his libido.

He shifted his stance and cleared his throat before the latter became too apparent.

She spun around, startled by the interruption. Her cheeks colored a becoming shade of pink when she realized what she'd been doing, and what he'd most likely seen.

She pressed a hand to her chest, as if to calm the rapid beating of her heart. "Garrett, I didn't expect you home so early." Her voice sounded breathless and incredibly sexy to his ears.

He turned down the radio, giving her a few extra seconds to recover her composure. "I'm home my normal time," he said with a nonchalant shrug.

She slanted him a sly, knowing glance as she resumed stirring the sauce. "What, did Rylan have a hot date tonight and couldn't cover for you?"

Was he that transparent? Apparently so. "Something like that," he muttered, shoving the tips of his fingers into the front pockets of his jeans. Anxious to change the topic away from *him*, he said, "You're quite a cook."

Her light laughter seemed to shimmer in the air around them. "You sound surprised."

"Pleasantly surprised," he admitted, moving closer to the stove to see what she'd concocted. Closer to her. "The casserole you left for supper last night was great, and whatever you made today smells delicious."

"Homemade spaghetti sauce and meatballs," she told him.

He took another long breath, expanding his lungs

with the delectable aroma. Oh, yeah, he'd died and gone to heaven, then was promptly jolted back to earth at the thought that Jenna was under the misconception that he *expected* her to cook. "Jenna, you don't have to do this. Making meals wasn't part of our agreement, or in your job description."

"I really don't mind." Her tone was as sincere as her gaze. Dipping the wooden spoon into the thick sauce, she held a sample up to his lips. "Taste it, and tell me what you think."

Her sweet smile, so filled with anticipation, was the only encouragement he needed to indulge in the fragrant delicacy she offered. He ate a bite, and groaned at the appetizing flavors that tantalized his taste buds. He could get used to this, he thought. Too easily, when the situation was very *temporary*.

"Incredible," he said, meaning it, just as his stomach growled loudly in agreement.

"I'll take that as a compliment." Eyes alight with silent laughter, she reduced the burner beneath the pot to a simmer. "I love to cook. I just never had much reason to be creative in the kitchen when it's been just me for so many years."

"You never cooked for your fiancé?"

She didn't avoid the personal question like he thought she might. "We ate out more often than in. It was one of the benefits of Sheldon's exclusive membership at the local country club." Her tone held a wry note. "He was a surgeon, and liked being the center of attention and enjoyed mingling with this colleagues. Having dinner there suited his purposes."

He regarded her intently. "And what kind of purpose did you serve, Jenna?"

She blinked at him, confusion creasing her soft features. "Excuse me?"

"I get the impression that you would have preferred intimate dinners for two at home, instead of being the center of attention, so I'm just wondering why two opposites like you and Sheldon would have wanted to marry in the first place."

She didn't swear undying love, but her spine did straighten with a bit of defense. "We weren't opposites, exactly." Her voice trailed off, and a troubled frown formed on her brow. "But we both knew what to expect from each other, and our relationship."

He wondered what kind of arrangement they'd had, because it was obvious that her surgeon-groom hadn't appreciated Jenna enough to come after her. And Garrett suddenly wanted to know *why*. He wrestled with his conscience, knowing he was stepping beyond boundaries he'd drawn for himself with this woman, but satiating his curiosity won.

"What happened to end your relationship with Sheldon at the altar?"

She glanced away, but not before he saw the panic in the depth of her eyes that his too personal question had kindled. "I told you before that I'm not the kind of woman Sheldon needs in his life."

His gaze narrowed on her. "And what kind of woman is that?"

"Someone far more respectable than I'll ever be."

Respectable. There was that word again. Without a doubt, her reply was an abbreviated version for something that had caused her great distress. A bride didn't walk up the aisle on her wedding day and at the last minute decide that she was less than respectable, or that there was a compatibility problem. Something had *happened,* something profound enough to make her believe she wasn't good enough for Sheldon and send her running to a small town to start a new life for herself.

Her anxiety was so palpable it struck a compassionate chord in Garrett. As much as he wanted to push the issue and discover whatever secret she seemed to be hiding, he just couldn't bring himself to be so insensitive. As he well knew with his own issues with Angela, some things were best left *private* and buried as deep as one's soul.

So, instead, he asked, "Where's Chelsea?"

Relief chased away the shadows that had clouded her eyes. "Upstairs changing into her swimsuit." Placing a lid on the pot of sauce, she managed a smile. "She wanted to play out in the pool for a little bit before supper, and before it cools off."

The sound of footsteps echoed from the other room, and then his daughter burst into the kitchen with a smile bright enough to rival the sun. "Daddy, you're home!" She launched herself into his arms for his daily hug. "Are you going to come swimming with us?" she asked hopefully.

He hadn't planned on spending any extra time with Jenna. In fact, he'd spent too much time with her already, had discovered more than he cared to know. His safest bet would be to say no and make up an excuse that would keep him indisposed until Jenna left for the day...

"Please?" Chelsea pleaded, as if sensing his indecision. "We can play Marco Polo tag since it's the three of us. We haven't played that in a long time.''

Despite his own reservations, Garrett found it difficult to refuse his daughter's simple request, especially when he had so little time to play and have fun with her.

He ruffled her silky hair affectionately. ''Give me a few minutes to change, pup, and I'll be there.''

Chelsea grinned. ''Last one in the pool is *it* for tag!''

Jenna was the last one outside to the pool, and thus dubbed ''it'' by Chelsea in a very gleeful tone of voice. She made a playful face at the young girl, but had no one to blame for her late arrival but herself, since she'd deliberately lagged behind in the kitchen.

She'd taken her time cleaning up the remnants of the meatballs and sauce she'd made while thinking about Garrett's personal questions. A part of her wished she *could* share the reason why her relationship with Sheldon had ended at the altar, of why she could never be the kind of woman Sheldon needed in his life. But fears and insecurities had a way of tangling her emotions into a huge knot in her chest, and kept her from confiding her most intimate secret to *anyone*.

She was finally beginning to feel as though she fit in somewhere, when she'd spent most of her life searching for acceptance. Every day that passed she experienced a deeper sense of belonging and security, and the risk of losing what little stability she'd gained was too high for her to trust anyone, especially Garrett, with the truth. He already harbored a grudge of some sort against his wife—she didn't need that mark against her, too.

Smiling as she watched Chelsea and Garrett toss a colorful beach ball back and forth in the shallow end, Jenna strolled across the deck to the umbrella table where Chelsea had stacked their towels. Her traitorous gaze strayed to Garrett's broad shoulders, the bare expanse of his back, and the play of muscles as he moved. His body was athletically honed, his skin smooth, tanned and gleaming from the sun. A pleasant rush of warmth tripped her pulse into a faster beat.

"How's the water?" she asked as she untied the knot securing the short skirt she'd wrapped around her waist earlier for modesty's sake.

Garrett caught the ball Chelsea threw his way and turned around to look at her. His dark, wet hair was slicked away from his face, making his relaxed features more prominent. "Cold at first, but it feels good once you're in."

The material fell away from her hips, and Garrett's gaze slowly traveled the length of her body intimately outlined in a black spandex swimsuit. His eyes turned hot with masculine appreciation, and even with the distance separating them she felt scorched from his brand of heat.

A twinge of self-consciousness immediately took up residence in her at his leisurely inspection, and she resisted the urge to put the skirt back on and cover her body. Lifting her chin a fraction to restore her sense of pride, she resolutely reminded herself that she'd been seen by hundreds, if not *thousands* of men, in a whole lot less.

But that knowledge didn't change the fact that

Garrett's opinion *mattered*. She cared about what he thought of her, and didn't want to be anything less than a feminine, *respectable* woman in his eyes.

Refusing to analyze that revelation too deeply, or why *his* acceptance was so important, she walked to the edge of the pool and tentatively stuck her big toe in the water, then feigned a brisk shiver. "I don't know, guys, that water is pretty chilly."

"Just jump in, Jenna," Chelsea said, splashing water over her bare feet and calves. "That's what we do, and then you don't have to think about how cold it is."

"It's the less painful alternative," Garrett agreed with a grin.

She backed up a few steps and eyed him dubiously. "What's my other option?"

His eyes glinted with a deviltry so opposite of the gruff, reserved man she was used to dealing with. "Me tracking you down and throwing you in." He started toward the pool's steps to come and get her.

This time, the tremor that coursed through her veins was very real. No way did she want to be carried in his arms, pressed against his chest, *clinging* to all that strength and masculinity. Before he could follow through on his threat, she took the plunge, literally, and jumped into the deep end of the pool. Cool water enveloped her, both shocking and refreshing at the same time. A few seconds later she broke the surface with a gasp for air and a chattering "Brrr."

Girlish giggles and rich chuckles drifted from the opposite end of the pool. Treading water to keep afloat, she narrowed her gaze on the duo who were indulging in too much amusement at her expense.

"I don't know what you two find so funny. I'm *it*," she reminded them, "so you'd best find a place to hide before I come and get you!"

She slipped beneath the water again, kicked off the bottom, and swam toward the shallow end. Eyes closed as the game dictated, she surfaced and called "Marco," and they answered, "Polo," giving her the only clue as to their whereabouts. Jenna deliberately avoided Garrett's deep voice and concentrated on Chelsea's, blindly following the direction of her voice until she tagged the little girl.

Then it was Chelsea's turn to seek Jenna and Garrett, and because they were much faster and stronger swimmers than Chelsea, Garrett let his daughter catch him before she grew tired and frustrated with the search. He tickled Chelsea until she laughed with delight and squealed for him to let her go.

"You need to get Jenna, Daddy!" Chelsea said, causing ripples in the water with her enthusiastic bouncing.

"I'm too fast and smart for your dad," Jenna teased, then quickly realized her mistake when she saw the challenging light in Garrett's eyes.

"We'll see about that," he murmured.

He ducked beneath the water to give them time to move to a new position, and though Jenna did her best to avoid Garrett, it took him less than two minutes to find and trap her at the side of the pool, right between the shallow and deep end. With every call of "Marco," and she answered "Polo," he closed the distance separating them, blocking any easy escape. The water lapped at his chest as he approached with eyes closed, his head cocked to the side to hear every sound she made. He looked too ready to spring in whichever direction she decided to take.

Though it was only a fun, harmless game, Jenna's heart beat frantically, with anticipation and a latent excitement. Three feet away from her, he called "Marco" again, and instead of issuing a reply, she decided to take her chances and try to dodge him.

Sliding silently beneath the water, she kicked off the side of the pool toward the deep end. Before she could reach her destination, a strong, muscular arm banded around her waist, bringing her flush against a hard, male body. Their bare legs tangled, silken skin against hair roughened skin, and her breasts swelled with instantaneous, sensual awareness.

She panicked, but not because he'd captured her. Her mind spun dizzily at the overwhelming sensation of being surrounded by such arousing heat. Reckless desire immediately followed, spurring her distress. She tried to pry away the hand he'd splayed against her stomach, but he held tight. With a hard kick, he propelled them both back up to the surface. As soon as their heads broke the water, she sucked air deep into her deprived lungs.

He eased them over to the side of the pool, which included more skin brushing together, and the feel of her bottom tucked against his thighs. There was nothing proper or modest about the deep, vital hunger that swept through her, the kind of *need* that could only lead to heartache with a remote man like Garrett Blackwell.

"Too fast and smart for me, huh?" he said into her ear, his low, rich voice mocking her. "Looks like I outsmarted the fox."

Oh, he'd more than proved his point, and she'd be careful of baiting him in the future. "And you nearly drowned me in the process!" she said, covering up her confusion with an indignant attitude.

She was playing with fire when it came to Garrett, a smoldering kind of attraction she wasn't prepared to deal with, not until she knew the direction of her future. And right now, her plans didn't include falling for a man who viewed her as more a responsibility and obligation, than anything else.

Shaken by what had happened and her uncontrollable reaction to him for the second time since that passionate kiss they'd shared, she struggled against his hold, and he finally released her. She quickly swam to the shallow end and climbed the steps out of the pool.

"Hey, Jenna, where are you going?" Chelsea asked, her spirits dampened by her sudden departure.

Grabbing a towel, she draped it over her shoulders, and summoned a smile for the little girl. "I need to get going, kiddo. I'll see you tomorrow, though." She forced herself to meet Garrett's gaze, which was guarded and unreadable, as if he hadn't just turned her inside out with a wanting so strong it defied her own reasoning. "All you need to do is add cooked spaghetti noodles to the sauce and meatballs I made, and your supper will be done."

She went inside and changed into her dry clothing. On the drive back to the boarding house she came to the realization that she was running again...running scared because of the feelings Garrett evoked.

CHAPTER SEVEN

JENNA glanced up from the invoices she was inputting into the computer as Lisa pushed open the door to Blackwell Engineering. The other woman waddled inside, a sparkle in her blue eyes and a wicker basket hooked over her arm.

"Hey, I thought you were supposed to be at home resting."

Lisa rolled her eyes as she approached the desk Jenna sat behind in the main reception area. "If my brother had his way, I'd be confined to the couch or my bed until these two are born." She lovingly patted her burgeoning stomach, which seemed to have grown in the few days since Jenna had last seen Lisa. "Garrett worries too much, more than my own husband does."

Jenna tapped a key on the computer to save the accounting document flickering on the screen. "It's hard to blame him when you look as though you're ready to have those babies any day now."

"I keep hoping, because these two are running out of space for their acrobatic moves." Lisa set the wicker basket on the corner of her desk and glanced surreptitiously into the open door of Garrett's office, which was situated behind Jenna. "I didn't see my brother's truck out front, so I'm assuming he's not here?"

"No. He's out on a bid until this afternoon."

"Good." Lisa dragged a chair over to Jenna's

110

desk, and plopped into it with an uncomfortable groan. "At least I can relax and enjoy myself without him fussing over me."

Jenna propped her chin in her hand and smiled. "So, what brings you by the office?"

"I was feeling cooped up and restless." She blew out an upward stream of breath that ruffled her black bangs. "I've cleaned the house, the babies' room is ready, and I'm tired of reading books. So, I made a couple of sandwiches and decided to eat out today. With you."

Jenna lifted a brow in surprise and glanced at the basket. "You made me lunch? How sweet."

"It was either that, or go crazy at home by myself." Opening the basket, she withdrew two wrapped sandwiches. "Which do you prefer, ham or turkey?"

"I'll take the ham," Jenna said, clearing off a corner of the desk so Lisa had room to unpack their lunch. Not only did she make sandwiches, but she'd also brought along a fruit salad, sodas, and homemade brownies for dessert.

"So, how is the boss treating you?" Lisa asked as they feasted on the fare she'd brought.

"Pretty good." Jenna bit into a juicy piece of watermelon and savored the delectable sweetness. "Garrett has been extremely patient with the few mistakes I've made."

"You've only been working here a week. You'll settle into the routine soon enough." Lisa chewed on a bite of sandwich and swallowed. "How are the afternoons with Chelsea?"

"Great." The little girl was precocious, and playful, and quickly finding a special spot in Jenna's heart. As was her father, she admitted. "Quite honestly, spending time with Chelsea is the best part of my day."

The second best part of her day was when Garrett arrived home in the evenings after work, though she was careful to avoid any more pool scenes with him. He might be all business in the office when he was there, but they'd settled into a comfortable, friendly routine at his house. Though Jenna never intended to stay once Garrett arrived home, Rylan and Chelsea insisted that she join them for the dinner she usually made. Now, her staying in the evenings had become an expected ritual.

Not that she minded, Jenna thought as she took a bite of her ham-and-cheese sandwich. Being a part of the Blackwell family filled that emptiness she'd carried within her for so long. The entire family accepted her unconditionally and made her feel like she belonged.

But at night, when she was alone in bed, the painful memory always seemed to tumble through her mind, reminding her of all the reasons why she needed to safeguard her heart against the tender feelings trying to weave their way inside. She still had no idea which direction her future was heading, and while the present here in Danby was a very comfortable place to be, she constantly feared her past would catch up to her again—and destroy whatever happiness she'd manage to accumulate.

But the most difficult part of both of her jobs was fighting her attraction to her gorgeous, sexy boss. The awareness that inevitably flared between her and Garrett when they were alone was a struggle to ignore. An accidental touch made her heart triple its beat. A warm, lingering look had the ability to make her weak in the knees and yearn for more of the sensual kisses she'd shared with Garrett.

But he remained a gentleman, and she tried to hold tight to the conviction that she was all wrong for him, no matter how flimsy the excuse sometimes felt. She couldn't be what he and Chelsea needed on a permanent basis. Despite yearning for more, Jenna knew and accepted that her part in their lives was as temporary as both of her jobs.

Finished with her sandwich, Jenna decided it was time to get back to work. "You know, since you're here, could you show me how to pull up the quarterly tax reports on the computer?"

"Ah, something to stimulate my brain," Lisa said with a grin. "I'd love to."

They cleaned up the remnants of their lunch, and Jenna moved Lisa's chair next to hers. She watched and listened as the other woman went over the tax report with her, then pointed out a few other short-cuts on other office-related procedures.

An hour later, Garrett walked in, and promptly frowned when he saw his sister sitting behind the desk, tapping away on the computer keyboard. "What are you doing here, Lisa?"

She smiled breezily. "I was just having lunch with Jenna."

He picked up his messages, his mouth pursed in disapproval. "It looks like you're *working* to me."

Lisa sighed, and stood. "Since the interrogator has returned, I think I'll take that as my cue to leave." She smiled at Jenna. "Getting out of the house was fun while it lasted."

Jenna rounded the desk behind Lisa, and handed

her the wicker basket. "Thank you for lunch, and for all your help."

"Any time..." Lisa sucked in a sharp breath. Her eyes widened in shock, and she grabbed at her stomach. "Oh, my," she whispered.

"What is it?" Jenna and Garrett asked at the same time.

Slowly, Lisa glanced down at the ground. Jenna and Garrett followed her gaze, finding a puddle of clear liquid around Lisa's sandaled feet.

Lisa looked back up as nervous laughter escaped her. "I think my water just broke."

Sitting in the waiting room at the hospital, Jenna sipped sweetened coffee from a foam cup as she watched Garrett pace a path in front of where she sat with Chelsea's sleepy head resting in her lap. A tired smile touched the corner of her mouth as she thought about everything that had led up to this moment.

Once Lisa's water broke at the office, Garrett had insisted on taking his sister immediately to the hospital, promising her they'd call her husband on Garrett's cell phone on the way so that Duane could meet them there when they arrived. Jenna shut down the office early, picked up Chelsea from camp, and met Garrett at the hospital. And here they'd waited for the past six hours. They'd eaten dinner in the cafeteria, Duane gave them regular updates on Lisa's progress, and all they could do was be patient and let the twins dictate when they were ready to make their appearance into the world.

Chelsea grew bored from the long wait and the uninteresting adult shows on the TV situated in the lounge. When she stretched out on the couch and rested her cheek on Jenna's thigh, Jenna knew it was only a matter of time before she fell asleep. Less than five minutes, to be exact.

Chelsea's father, however, was a bundle of restless energy. Garrett couldn't sit for long without popping back up and resuming his nervous pacing. Jenna didn't mind watching him, not when he was such a fine male specimen to look at—one who moved with such lithe, athletic grace. His body was muscular, but lean, and he filled out a pair of jeans very nicely—front and back, she thought, as he pivoted away from her.

Reaching the end of the small room, he whirled around and stalked back toward her, his gaze a dark, stormy shade of blue. "If Lisa would have been at home resting where she belongs, this never would have happened."

It was the same argument he'd been issuing since she'd arrived at the hospital. "Lisa would have gone into labor at home, Garrett," she tried to reason, not for the first time. "Those twins are *ready* to be born."

He stabbed his fingers through the dark, tousled hair that he'd been abusing all evening. "But she's not due for another three weeks."

"From what I've heard, twins are usually early. And from what I know, babies are very unpredictable when it comes to keeping to their due date." Finished with her coffee, she handed Garrett her empty cup.

He pitched it into a nearby trash, then resumed his agitated pattern across the waiting room. He glanced at his watch, and his frown deepened. "What's taking them so long?"

"Babies come in their own time, when they're good and ready." Jenna stroked her hand over Chelsea's head and through her straight, silky hair, reveling in the soft texture so opposite of her wild curls. "Surely you know that from when Chelsea was born."

Releasing a taut stream of breath, Garrett dropped into the chair across from where Jenna sat on the couch, forcing himself to relax. The tension from his body eased, but Jenna's comment caused his mind to drift to the past, and the day Chelsea had been born. Yes, he'd learned a lot about babies that day, more than he'd ever believe possible. He'd discovered just how deeply Angela had deceived him.

His stomach clenched as he recalled the gamut of emotions he'd endured that fateful day that had changed his entire life…joy that Chelsea had been born a strong and fully developed infant. Anger that a woman he'd pledged eternal devotion to and had trusted could betray him the way she had. And resignation because he knew he'd *never* shirk the responsibility that had become his. But despite the circumstances of Chelsea's birth, he'd never once regretted having her in his life.

His gaze flickered to Jenna, another woman who roused a variety of feelings within him. Tenderness. Caring. And the kind of responsibility that had led him to trouble in the past. But unlike Angela, Jenna was honest and genuine. She showered affection on his daughter, made his life brighter and more manageable with her presence, and reminded him on a daily basis of how much he'd once wanted a wife and family of his own.

Resisting her was becoming more and more difficult.

Duane burst through the double doors leading from the maternity ward, causing Garrett to jump up from his seat and leave his wayward thoughts behind.

Dressed in standard hospital scrubs and wearing a huge grin, Lisa's husband gave a loud whoop and threw a victory punch in the air. "We've got ourselves a healthy boy and girl."

Relief poured through Garrett, giving way to a broad grin of his own. He shook his brother-in-law's hand. "Congratulations, to the four of you."

Jenna woke up Chelsea to give her the exciting news that she now had two cousins, then stood and hugged Duane. "I'm so happy for both you and Lisa."

"When do we get to see the babies, Uncle Duane?" Chelsea asked, suddenly wide awake, bright-eyed, and eager.

Duane laughed and tweaked Chelsea's nose. "They'll be cleaned up and in the nursery in about half an hour for you to see," he told her. "When Aunt Lisa gets home in a few days, then you can hold them."

"How *is* Lisa doing?" Garrett asked.

"Great, but she's exhausted." He shook his head, his expression awed. "Jacob and Janet are going to be a handful, I can already tell."

Garrett chuckled his agreement. "Say goodbye to sleeping through the night for the next year," he teased, then grew serious. "We're going to see the babies in the nursery, then we'll be on our way. Give Lisa our love, tell her to get some rest tonight, and we'll be by in the morning to see her.''

Duane nodded, already on his way back through the double doors to return to his wife. ''Will do.''

''Aren't they just the sweetest things you've ever seen?''

Hearing the longing in Jenna's voice, Garrett glanced from the nursery window where they were watching the twins—one swaddled in a blue blanket, the other in pink—and looked at Jenna's profile. Her features were soft with yearning, her smile wistful, and he felt reeled in by that emotion-filled expression in ways that startled him.

Ignoring the warmth pervading his chest, he returned his attention to the babies. ''Yeah, they are pretty darn cute,'' he said, his voice low and husky.

Standing between Garrett and Jenna, Chelsea lifted up on her tiptoes to get a better look at her cousins. She promptly frowned. ''How come their faces are all red and wrinkly?''

Jenna chuckled and gave Chelsea an affectionate squeeze. ''Newborns look that way for a few days,'' she said before Garrett could attempt a simple explanation for his daughter. ''I'm sure by the time we see them at your aunt Lisa's all those wrinkles will be gone.''

Chelsea contemplated that for a moment, then tipped her head up toward Jenna. ''When are you going to have a baby?''

Jenna's eyes grew round, and Garrett watched her absently press a hand to her flat belly. She quickly recovered from the initial shock of Chelsea's guileless question. "Maybe someday when I find myself a prince charming who will have me."

Not only did she appeal to his daughter's imagination with her fairy-tale type reply, but Garrett was once again reminded of the night he'd met Jenna, and how she'd told him how she wished to marry a prince charming and live happily ever after. She deserved that kind of stability and happiness—any woman did, but he wasn't the man to provide it, no matter how much Jenna tempted him to explore the attraction between them. He didn't have it in him to offer any woman those kinds of promises, not after the way Angela had tapped him dry. Even as his mind accepted the lecture, a part of his soul couldn't deny just how perfectly Jenna fit into his life, and Chelsea's. She was slowly becoming more than a damned attractive responsibility he'd gotten himself tangled up with.

An impish grin creased the corner of Jenna's mouth, making her beauty mark lift with the gesture. "I'd like to have at least three or four babies someday," she told Chelsea.

"Wow!" Chelsea breathed, shifting from one foot to the other. "Your tummy would be twice as big as Aunt Lisa's!"

Jenna laughed, the sound light and lilting. "Well, I'd like to have them one at a time, not all at once." She ruffled Chelsea's hair.

His daughter went back to watching the twins, who were squirming in their blankets and waking up from their brief naps. With amusement still shimmering in her periwinkle eyes over Chelsea's rapt fascination with babies, Jenna's gaze found his.

He returned her smile, finding it very easy to do,

and shoved his fingers into the front pockets of his jeans. "So, you want that many babies, huh?"

Though his question was a genuinely curious one, there was nothing he could do to stop the mental image that suddenly formed in his mind, of making a baby with Jenna, of her warm and willing beneath him, and the soft sighs she'd make when they were finally entwined as one...

"Yeah, I do want that many babies." Her soft voice brought him back to reality with a much needed jolt. "I grew up without any brothers or sisters, and I always wished I had a sibling or two to play with."

"Or argue and fight with," he added wryly, propping his shoulder against the glass enclosed wall of the nursery.

"That, too." She touched the tips of her fingers to the window, as if to reach out and somehow feel connected to the babies within. "Being an only child, I always felt so...alone."

He wondered if Chelsea ever felt that way, alone and lonely, then told himself that his daughter now had two cousins to fill any sibling void, or any yearning she might have for a playmate. "Did Sheldon want kids?"

Jenna's shoulder lifted in a shrug that didn't match the nonchalance he suspected she was striving for. "I'm sure we would have had a family."

"Because it was expected of you, and all part of that purpose you served for Sheldon?"

She stared at him for a long moment, the depths of her eyes brimming with a wealth of sadness. He expected her to turn away, to skirt the issue he'd addressed. Surprisingly, she didn't.

"We both served a purpose for each other," she admitted, and didn't sound proud of that fact. She took a deep, fortifying breath. "Garrett...Sheldon was my chance at respectability."

Her voice was so small, a mere, aching whisper, but there was no denying what he'd heard. Confusion assailed him, even as her words grabbed compassionately at his heart. "And what makes you believe you aren't respectable?" he asked in an equally low voice.

She attempted an unsteady smile that did nothing to banish the shadows in her eyes. "You're better off not knowing."

And then, as if it hurt too much to look at him, she turned back to the twins in the nursery, and bent close to his daughter. "Look, Chelsea," she said, pointing to the baby bundled in blue, who in his restless squirming had managed to loosen the blanket around his arms. His little fist flailed wildly in the air. "I think Jacob is waving at you."

"I saw him!" Chelsea exclaimed excitedly, and grabbed for Garrett's hand. "Daddy, did you see that?"

"Yeah, pup, I saw him," he fibbed, his voice gravelly. Truth be told, the only thing he could *see* at the moment, *feel* at the moment, was Jenna's pain.

And that wasn't a good thing. Not at all.

CHAPTER EIGHT

"I'M SORRY I'm so late."

Jenna closed the romance novel she was reading and set it on the small table next to the couch as Garrett walked into the living room. It was twenty after eight in the evening, much longer than she normally stayed to watch Chelsea, but she didn't mind. She'd much rather be at Garrett's than sequestered in her quiet, lonely room at the boarding house.

"No need to apologize." She welcomed him with a warm smile. "Everything go okay with your meeting in St. Louis?"

"Yes." He sat in the chair next to her, his expression relaxed and pleased. "It took longer than I thought to hash out the numbers with the estimate I presented, but Blackwell Engineering got the job."

Excited for him, she reached out and placed her hand over his arm without giving the gesture much thought until after the fact. "That's wonderful news."

He inhaled sharply, and his gaze jumped from her hand to her eyes as sensual currents flared between them like wildfire. Her stomach dipped. Beneath her fingers, she felt his hot skin, the flex of muscles that indicated her casual caress affected him on a much deeper level than the supportive touch it had meant to be.

It had been this way for the past few weeks— both of them avoiding close proximity, and dodging their simmering attraction in their mutual attempt to maintain a professional, business-like relationship. But there was no denying the steady, spiraling need blossoming within Jenna—a desire that was becoming more and more difficult to resist.

Following the safe route of protecting her heart from those emotions, she withdrew her hand the same time she tucked away what wasn't hers to take.

Garrett visibly struggled to regain his shaken composure, too. "It's quiet in here," he said after a long moment had passed. Cocking his head to the side, he listened more intently. "Where's Chelsea?"

Ah, an enjoyable, distracting topic. "Your daughter had a long, busy day. I put her to bed at eight after her bath. She was out in minutes."

He leaned back in his chair and folded his hands casually behind his head. The lamplight beside him cast a golden hue around his head and highlighted his handsome features. "And Rylan?"

"You have to ask?" She grinned indulgently, and tucked a springy curl of hair behind her ear. "He's out with Emma."

"Of course." His mouth twitched with amusement. "So, what did you and Chelsea do this afternoon?"

Their easy conversation was comfortable and predictable. There was a simplicity and normalcy about their evening ritual, one that made her feel like she and Garrett had been following this same routine for years, instead of only a few weeks. Except at the end of the night they parted ways, instead of her taking his hand and following him up those stairs to his bedroom.

But for as much as she craved the magic she was

certain the two of them would make together, she also knew how complicated making love with this man would be.

Feeling a warm heat infuse her cheeks at her private thoughts, she reined in the overwhelming desire that was becoming increasingly difficult to ignore. "After I picked up Chelsea from camp, we went to Lisa's and saw the twins."

A lazy smile curved his mouth. "Everyone settled in okay?"

"Yeah." She curled her legs up onto the couch next to her, and his warm gaze slid to her calves, bared by the summer dress she'd worn. She drew a breath to put a stop to the quivering deep in her belly. "Chelsea held both Jacob and Janet, which was a huge thrill for her."

"Sounds like she'll be a big help to Lisa when my sister is back to watching Chelsea again."

Garrett's idle comment served to remind Jenna how temporary her presence in his life was, and how much she was beginning to dread the thought of no longer seeing him and Chelsea on a daily basis once her job was over.

"Yeah, she will," Jenna agreed, and cleared the sudden tightness from her throat. Toying with the hem of her dress, she transferred her gaze to the photo album sitting on the coffee table in front of them. "Garrett..." She paused, uncertain how to broach the subject that had been on her mind since viewing the pictures in that album. "Seeing the twins today made Chelsea want to see her own baby book."

"That's fine." He shrugged as if she'd brought

up an inconsequential matter. "She's looked through it before."

"And does she always ask questions about her mother?"

"Sometimes." He shifted in his chair, suddenly seeming uncomfortable. "She knows that Angela died when she was almost two, and like I told you before, she doesn't remember much about her mother. Not that there is much to recall."

The bitterness creeping into his voice didn't deter Jenna's purpose. "I found the pictures...interesting."

His brows furrowed, and his body stiffened in a way that was undeniably defensive. "Interesting in what way?"

"In all the pictures with you, your wife, and Chelsea, Angela looks as though she'd rather be anywhere else but *there*."

"That's because she *would have* rather been anywhere else but *here*." He rubbed his fingers along his jaw, the agitated gesture reflecting a deeper turmoil. "Angela was never the maternal type, and being married and living in this small town wasn't exciting enough for her. She didn't care who knew how miserable she was, either."

Then why had they gotten married? Jenna swallowed the curious question that rushed forward, and said instead, "I also noticed that there isn't really much of a resemblance between Angela and Chelsea, or even you." The contrasts in complexions and coloring was obvious, and puzzling. "Where did Chelsea get such fair hair and those green eyes when Angela and everyone I've met in your family has black hair and blue eyes?"

His jaw clenched tight, and a cynical light glinted in his eyes. "I always assumed Chelsea must look like her father."

Startled and confused by his peculiar reply, and certain she'd heard him incorrectly, she frowned. "Excuse me?" She'd been expecting a more logical explanation—that some distant relative on Garrett's side of the family possessed those fair traits Chelsea had inherited.

With a low, sworn oath, Garrett stood and crossed the living room to the window and stared out at the darkness of night. Jenna watched him go, the air suddenly vibrating with the kind of tension that preceded a violent tempest.

Suppressing an apprehensive shiver, she took a huge risk and stepped into the eye of the storm. His dark comment had dredged up too many issues for her to dismiss so easily. "Garrett?" she asked, her voice quiet but firm, even as her heart beat wildly in her chest. "What do you mean you assumed Chelsea must look like her father?"

He flinched, the muscles across his back bunching with the quick movement, as if she'd whipped him with the very words he'd so carelessly spoken moments before. He blew out a harsh breath and hung his head, and for a reason that alluded her, she wanted him to trust her with whatever burden he carried—even as she realized she was holding tight to a secret of her own.

Finally, he glanced over his shoulder and looked at her. His initial anger had ebbed into a resignation that touched his features and glimmered in his eyes. "I'm not Chelsea's real father." A bittersweet smile twisted his mouth. "Chelsea doesn't have an ounce of Blackwell blood running through her veins."

Jenna stared at him in stunned silence.

He shook his head, and swore beneath his breath. "I'm sorry," he said gruffly. "I never should have said anything. Other than my family, you're the only one who knows the truth about Chelsea, and I'd prefer if you kept it to yourself."

It was a request she'd respect. "Why did you tell me?"

"I don't have a reason that makes a whole lot of sense," he admitted. "I just thought you'd understand."

She understood, more than he'd ever realize. "Will you tell me what happened?"

He came around to her side of the couch and sat beside her, resting his forearms on his thighs. His posture was stiff, and she ached to reach out and touch him, but didn't dare. She waited quietly, calmly, for him to make the decision of whether or not he wanted to talk about the past.

After what seemed like an eternity, he rewarded her patience. "I met Angela much the same way I met you."

"She ran out on her wedding day and ended up at Leisure Pointe?"

He chuckled, the smooth, deep sound lifting the strained moment that had settled over them. "No. Let me rephrase that. She was in need of help, and I rescued her, so to speak."

She grabbed one of the couch's throw pillows and hugged it close. "Just like you rescued me," she murmured, having learned that this man would never turn his back on a woman in need.

"Exactly." His gaze remained riveted on some spot on the floor between his booted feet. "Angela's car died on her just outside of Danby, and I was on my way home from St. Louis when she waved me down. I couldn't leave a woman standing on the side of the road when she was obviously stranded, so I pulled over, intending to get her the help she needed, and be on my way."

He tipped his head her way, and she saw the self-condemnation in his eyes. "She was from St. Louis, too, and very beautiful and sophisticated in a way that suckered me right in. When she decided to stay overnight in Danby while the garage in town fixed her car, she insisted on buying me dinner as a way of thanking me for my help. I was twenty-one at the time, and she was flirtatious and aggressive, and damn difficult to refuse."

It wasn't hard for Jenna to figure out where Angela's flagrant advances had led. "You had an affair with her?"

"Yep." He released a long, heavy sigh. "Five weeks later, she tells me she's pregnant, and I married her without a second thought. I was raised to always do the right thing, to be responsible for my actions, and there was no doubt in my mind that I wanted my baby to have both a mother and father."

"But the baby wasn't yours," she whispered.

"I figured that out when I thought Chelsea was born two months premature," he said, his tone wry. "When the doctor assured me that she was a healthy, full-term baby, everything finally made sense. I confronted Angela with the truth, and she admitted that I wasn't the father of her baby. She'd married me so she wouldn't have the child out of wedlock, and for security. Except she was never happy being married, and she hated it here in Danby.''

She fingered the fringe on the pillow in her lap. ''And Chelsea doesn't know the truth, either, does she?''

''She doesn't ever need to know.'' His eyes glowed with a fierce, paternal light. ''She's been *mine* since the day she was born, and I love her. Whoever fathered Chelsea never gave a damn about her, according to Angela, and that's why Angela duped me into marrying her.''

He shoved his fingers through his thick hair, mussing the strands. ''Things were never the same between Angela and I after that, not that our marriage was great to begin with. But her deception added an extra strain to our relationship. Less than two years after Chelsea was born, Angela asked for a divorce.''

Jenna remained quiet, knowing there was more.

''I grew up in a close-knit family filled with the love and warmth of two parents, and I was loathe to grant Angela's wish, but I did it anyway because we were both miserable.'' His mouth thinned into a harsh line. ''But I wasn't about to give her full custody of Chelsea like she wanted, when I knew damn well it was nothing more than a vindictive attempt to hurt me. Chelsea is, and always will be, *my* daughter. My name is on her birth certificate, and I was prepared to fight for her. And I did, even though it meant a nasty, bitter court battle.''

She tugged on her bottom lip with her teeth, unable to imagine the emotional pain he'd endured, all for his daughter. She hurt for him, that his wife had treated him so callously when he was a man of honor and integrity.

"And then, before the custody suit was settled, Angela was killed in a car accident," Garrett went on. "Her brakes failed and she slammed into a tree, and because of the obvious animosity between the two of us, I was automatically questioned by the authorities as a suspect in the crash."

She sucked in a shocked breath. "Oh, Garrett..." The disbelief in her voice was apparent.

His expression was as grim as the circumstances he'd mentioned. "As you can imagine, the town had a field day with that scandal. Nobody really believed that I'd do such a thing, but it was fuel for gossip, and I was the center of speculation until my name was cleared."

It suddenly hurt for Jenna to draw air into her lungs. She found herself holding tight to the pillow in her arms, realizing that the disgrace Angela had brought upon Garrett and his family was all too similar to her own ability to do the same if her past ever caught up to her. And not only would the shocking secret she harbored cause Garrett additional resentment if she dragged him into the middle of it, but Jenna's biggest fear was that she'd lose all that she'd gained in the short time she'd been in Danby. Acceptance, and a sense of belonging like nothing she'd ever known in her life.

But even as she tried to calm her own apprehension, she couldn't ignore the pain she saw in Garrett's deep blue eyes, couldn't stop the impulse to offer him comfort and understanding for all he'd endured. She did the only thing she knew to ease his misery—she pressed her palm to his stubbled cheek and gave him the solace of a gentle, caring caress. "I'm sorry you had to go through all that," she murmured.

He caught her hand when she would have pulled away, holding her captive. Her heart thumped hard in her chest. He said nothing, just stared at her for a long moment. His thumb stroked the rapid pulse in her wrist, heating her skin, melting her resolve to keep him at arm's length.

She gripped the pillow like a lifeline.

The mood between them subtly shifted, the atmosphere charging with a lush, breathtaking sensuality. Belatedly, she realized she never should have been so bold as to touch him, especially when she knew how such a simple gesture with Garrett could lead to such arousing consequences.

There was nothing simple about the need swirling between them, nothing ordinary about how much she wanted him.

"Garrett?" Her voice quivered with a combination of longing and uncertainty, as did her body.

"I want to kiss you," he murmured huskily, his words a sweet, seductive drug that made her lethargic, and forget all logical reason. "I want to taste something good and pure...I want something to make me *forget*."

She swallowed hard, unable to deny his request. And she wanted to forget, too, about her past, and just how easily she could bring yet another scandal down upon his family. She wanted to forget, just for a while, that she could never be the kind of woman he needed in his life.

His nearness, his warm male scent, overloaded

her senses, yet she tried to maintain a hold on her sanity. "We shouldn't."

"We've both been denying this for too long." He turned more fully toward her and brought her hand to his chest so she could feel his strong heartbeat and the overwhelming heat of him. "I've been going crazy trying to resist you. Just one kiss…"

His head slowly lowered, and he skimmed his mouth across hers—soft and slow and persuasive. His tongue teased her lower lip, and with a soft moan, her lashes fluttered closed and she surrendered to him. He slipped inside, deep and hot, and she openly welcomed him, kissing him back with the same thrilling excitement.

He stroked a hand across her shoulder, down her back, and over her hip. When he encountered the pillow still between them, he tugged her only anchor away and tossed it to the floor. The only thing left to hold on to was *him*, and she wrapped her arms around his neck. Gradually, he eased her closer, effortlessly shifted their bodies, and gently pulled her beneath him on the couch. Like warmed honey, she flowed to his will, too caught up in the moment, the man, and the wondrous feelings he evoked to contemplate where this one kiss had led…from a gesture of comfort, to a sensual embrace that made her feel safe, secure, and incredibly desirable.

His mouth still fused with hers, he stretched out over her, and settled a hard thigh between hers. Their hips meshed intimately, and she felt his arousal, which inflamed her even more. Her breasts ached where his chest crushed against the sensitive tips. Her legs tingled. Never had she experienced such consuming, physical pleasure, such emotional need and hunger for a man. And she wanted it to go on and on...

One hand tangled in her hair, while his other deftly undid the buttons down the front of her dress until the material parted and his palm covered her full breast through the lacy webbing of her bra. She gasped as her nipple beaded against his touch and a liquid warmth infused her veins. His mouth left hers to drift along her jaw, then trail kisses down her throat. With a soft sigh, she arched her neck, enjoying the sensations igniting within her...then panicked when his open mouth, his heated breath, glided across the upper slope of her breast and headed toward the taut, aching center.

For as badly as she wanted Garrett, for as much as she knew giving herself to him would be incredible on so many levels, she wasn't ready to relinquish the one last bit of respectability she had to call her own. *Not without love.*

He seemed to sense her doubts without her having to verbally express them. He stopped his exploration and lifted his head, his velvet-blue eyes latching on to her gaze. With a tenderness that belied the sexual tension strumming through his body, he restored the front of her dress back to its original order.

A knowing smile tipped the corner of his mouth, and he gently dragged his knuckles down her cheek. "Too much, too soon?"

Incapable of speech, she drew a deep breath and nodded.

He sat up, and helped her back to a sitting position. Her face felt flushed, and she smoothed nervous fingers over the skirt of her dress, giving the task her full concentration. He grabbed her hand,

and her attention, and she had no choice but to look into his eyes and see the deeper layers of emotion tonight had revealed. She was stunned to realize that she hadn't been the only one who'd felt the substantial change between them.

"Jenna...I'm tired of fighting whatever's between us. You're the first woman I've wanted, *really* wanted, in a long time, and I'm thinking...maybe we could take this, *us,* slow and easy and just see where things go?"

Her first instinct prompted her to say no, to listen to the voice inside her head that told her she wasn't the right woman for him. That allowing him any deeper into her heart would be plain foolish.

But it was the glimmer of hope in his expression, and her own craving for everything he offered that gave her the courage to say the one word that would let her pretend, for a little while, that this particular prince charming was hers.

"Yes," she whispered, and hoped her own selfish yearning didn't end up hurting the two people who'd come to mean so much to her.

CHAPTER NINE

"I CAUGHT one, I caught one!" Chelsea's gleeful voice sent a nearby flock of birds scattering in half a dozen different directions. The young girl stood by the shore of the lake where they'd spent the afternoon on a Sunday picnic, a fishing pole in her hand and a huge smile wreathing her face. "Look, Daddy, Jenna, the fish is so big and I got him all by myself!" Chelsea tried to subdue the squirming trout, who kept slipping through her hands.

Jenna's light, carefree laughter wrapped around Garrett, as warm and soft as the afternoon breeze. He was getting used to the sweet sound, and even more used to spending quality time with Jenna. Easing to his feet from the blanket they'd been sharing beneath a large shady tree, he started toward his daughter.

"Good job, pup." The fish was only about five inches long, but the largest one Chelsea had ever snagged by herself. "Must have been that tasty worm you put on the hook."

"I think you're right." She puffed out her chest importantly, proud of her accomplishment. "Can we cook him for dinner tonight?"

Garrett grinned down at her. "He looks like a one-meal kind of fish. We can cook him for *your* dinner." Unhooking the fish, he tossed it into a nearby bucket, then washed his hands in the lake.

"I'll clean him when we get home. Do you want to try and catch another one?"

Chelsea thought for a moment, her pink, freckled nose scrunching up in thought. "Maybe later. Can I go pick some of those wildflowers over in that field?"

Like any normal eight-year-old, she'd grown bored with her current activity and wanted to move on to something new. "Sure, so long as you stay close by."

Her expression turned adorably impish. "I want to make a crown of daisies for Jenna," she whispered secretively, then skipped off, her silky blond hair shimmering in the sun.

When he returned to the blanket and Jenna, she was stretched out on her back, looking up at the sky and fluffy, white clouds drifting past. She looked breathtakingly beautiful with her wheat-colored hair spread around her head in a crush of wild curls, her eyes glimmering with happiness, and her features relaxed. As he eased down on his stomach beside her and propped himself up on his forearms so he was inches away, he decided he could watch her for hours and never grow tired of the view.

A month ago, he never would have thought himself capable of feeling such whimsical sentiments about a woman. Especially not Jenna. But ever since that night over a week ago when he'd told her about Angela, they'd formed a fragile bond, one that was growing in strength with each passing day they spent together.

He found himself constantly infused with the need to be with her, to see her smile and hear her voice at work, and to come home to her in the evenings.

At night, after supper and Chelsea was tucked into bed, it took little encouragement from him to coax Jenna to stay a while longer. They'd sit together on the couch eating popcorn and watching TV, or talk about inconsequential things and share personal, intimate conversations. Their relationship remained private, but had most definitely turned romantic and meaningful on both physical and emotional levels.

He threaded his fingers through her sun-kissed hair, and rubbed the fragrant strands between his fingers. She turned her head and smiled at him, and just like that, desire coiled low in his belly.

There were always kisses and caresses during their time alone, accompanied by deep, needy moans and soft sighs of pleasure. He couldn't seem to get enough of her, and felt like a kid in the throes of his first crush. But keeping to his slow and easy promise, he always ended things before they escalated out of control.

While a part of him remained cautious and reserved about his feelings for Jenna, his heart was beginning to soften, allowing this warm and caring woman into that cold, dark place Angela had carved out with her betrayal. Maybe, just maybe, in finding a lost bride he'd also found a woman who complemented him more perfectly than any other.

A woman he could trust with his heart and soul.

"Hey," she said in a husky tone that captured his attention and banished that startling revelation from his mind. "I haven't seen one of these frowns in a while. No serious thoughts allowed today." She reached up and smoothed her fingers over his creased brow.

"Yes, ma'am." Grabbing her hand, he placed a

kiss in the center of her palm. "Are you having a good time?"

"It's been wonderful and fun and so relaxing." A contented sigh escaped her. "Thank you for asking me to come today. I really enjoyed being with you and Chelsea and having a picnic and watching her fish. She's so lucky to have you as a father, you know that?"

Even though Jenna knew the truth about Chelsea's parentage, she didn't make him feel any less than Chelsea's true father. And he was, in every way that counted and mattered.

"I think I'm equally lucky to have her." He turned his head to look out toward the field of wild-flowers and found that Chelsea had gotten distracted from her original purpose and was chasing a butter-fly. He smiled. "Life would be so ordinary without her in it."

Jenna's fingers brushed along his cheek, and he glanced back at her. Something near the vicinity of his heart tripped at the wistfulness in her eyes.

"I wish my own father would have felt a tenth of what you do for Chelsea," she whispered.

Her melancholy was so strong, her feelings toward a man who'd never been a part of her life so powerful, it made him ache deep inside for her and what she'd never had. "How come you never knew your father?"

She cast her gaze back up to the sky, giving him the distinct impression that she'd avoid answering the question if she could.

He wasn't about to let her off that easy, not after the way he'd opened up to her about Angela. With the light touch of a finger, he tipped her face back to him. "Tell me, sweetheart," he coaxed gently. "I wouldn't ask if I honestly wasn't interested in your answer. I want to know who Jenna Phillips is, where she came from, and where she's been. Is that so much to ask?"

She worried her bottom lip with her teeth, and her searching eyes seemed to radiate a dozen different kind of insecurities. Garrett even thought he detected a tinge of fear.

Then she shook her head and said very softly, "No, that's not too much to ask."

He grinned and nibbled on the tips of her fingers, trying to lighten the moment. "Then indulge me."

A smile flirted around the corners of her luscious mouth. "You're hard to refuse, you know that?"

He lifted a teasing brow. "Are you saying I'm irresistible?"

"Yeah, I guess maybe I am." Her slender fingers pushed back a lock of hair that had fallen across his forehead, another stall tactic, he guessed. But they had the rest of the afternoon together, and he was willing to wait patiently for her to tell him her story.

After a long quiet moment passed, she finally spoke. "My mother was seventeen when she got pregnant with me, and the guy she was seeing at the time denied being the father because he didn't want the responsibility of having a kid. He completely shut her out of his life, and that was the end of his involvement with her, and me." She lowered her gaze, but there was no mistaking the glimpse of sadness he'd seen in the depth of her eyes. "From what my mom told me when I asked, her parents weren't happy about the situation, either, and they weren't very supportive of her decision to keep me. In fact, they kicked her out of the house and refused to help her.''

He stared at her in shock, unable to comprehend how a family could shun one of their own. ''What did your mother do?''

''Well, she had me on her own, and I'm so grateful she did keep me instead of putting me up for adoption. But the decision cost my mother so much emotionally, and literally changed the direction of her life and future.''

He rolled to his side, closer to her, and supported his head against his palm. Behind them, he could hear Chelsea singing an off-tune song as she played. ''How so?''

''She never really recovered from my father's rejection.'' She drew a deep, stabilizing breath. ''When I was born, she was living in Wisconsin and struggling to support herself, and me. And then she met a man named Wade. I don't remember much about him, but she ended up following him here to Missouri. Shortly after that, he left her and we were back on our own again. Unfortunately for my mother, that cycle with men repeated itself many times over the years.''

Still holding her hand, he laced their fingers together, not at all surprised to realize how right the intimacy felt with her. ''Did your mother ever remarry?''

She shook her head. ''No, but not for a lack of not wanting to. Her relationships never lasted long, and it was always the guy who left her. She spent her life looking for a man who'd give her the kind of security and stability she craved.''

''And respectability,'' he added without conscious thought, finally realizing where Jenna's own need for the same stemmed from.

She appeared startled that he'd delved so deep, but didn't deny his claim. "Yes, and she wanted the same for me." She swallowed, her voice tight with emotion when she continued. "But my biggest fear is that I'm going to end up just like my mother... alone and lonely."

Compelled to convince her otherwise, he leaned over her, filling her vision with nothing but *him*. Framing her face between his big palms, he stared intently into her eyes. "You're one of the most respectable women I know, Jenna." She tried to avert her gaze, as if she didn't believe his statement, but he wouldn't let her look away. "Despite being stubborn and independent, you're caring and generous, and I'm beginning to think that Sheldon was a fool to let you go."

Her chin tipped up defensively. "Sheldon had his reasons for ending our relationship."

There was so much more. He could see the shadows of pain in her eyes and expression, but suspected if he pushed, she'd withdraw. Whatever it was that had sent her running on her wedding day, he wanted her to trust him with the truth.

And so he said nothing. He slid a hand into her soft curls, and smiled when a ringlet coiled tightly around his finger, just as she was ensnaring a large portion of his heart. He rested his other hand on her waist and slowly eased her closer, until her breasts brushed his chest and he leaned over her, blocking her from Chelsea's view. Her eyes darkened, and his pulse pounded as the air around them changed, charging with an intimate awareness that grew in intensity with each second that passed.

She dampened her bottom lip with her tongue, drawing his gaze to her mouth. The impulse to kiss her was too strong to resist. Yielding to the searing need, he slowly lowered his head; her lashes fell half-mast, and her lips automatically parted in expectation.

For as much as he wanted to devour her, he let her initiate the gradual melding of lips, the first touch of their tongues, and followed whatever pace she dictated. Having shared many kisses, they were beyond the shy, tentative stage. Now, they were in sync and totally in tune to what excited the other.

It didn't take much to arouse him where Jenna was concerned. She was so giving, so uninhibited in her response to him, that his entire body came alive with wanting her, sometimes with a mere look. But he kept a tight rein on his desire, all too aware that his daughter was nearby and this embrace could go no further than a kiss.

But oh, man, what a kiss it was...slow and lazy and soulful. Deep and drugging. She tasted like the sweet, luscious strawberries they'd eaten with their lunch, and she expressed her need for him in a way that would have brought him to his knees if he'd been standing. She melted into him so trustingly, filling him with an amazing sense of completeness. The delicious languor infusing his veins, the rightness of this woman in his arms, all combined to heighten his pleasure.

With a soft sigh, she ended the kiss, and let one of her hands drift down to feel his heartbeat beneath her palm. She met his gaze with a feminine smile on her pink, well-kissed lips. "I could get very used to this."

He grinned back at her. "Yeah, me, too."

"Jenna!" Chelsea called enthusiastically, her voice echoing their way as she approached. "I've got something for you."

Jenna started at the sound of his daughter's voice, then attempted to untangle herself from his arms. He held her captive with the hand still grasping her waist.

She shot him a desperate look. "Now's not the time to be playful," she whispered vehemently. "Chelsea's going to see us!"

He watched as her cheeks flushed a deeper shade of pink. "What's wrong with Chelsea seeing us together?"

Her mouth opened, then shut again. She stared at him, seemingly unable to find a solid argument to counter him with, but there was no mistaking the question swirling in her eyes. *What, exactly, did he mean by that?*

He inhaled a deep breath, and put complete faith in his feelings for Jenna. "I don't want us to sneak around to be together." There was no other woman he wanted in his life, he was tired of fighting his feelings for Jenna, and he wanted everyone to know that she was his. "And I don't want to hide the fact that you and I are seeing each other."

Shock enveloped her features. While she absorbed that unexpected overture, he sat up and pulled her to a sitting position next to him just as his daughter arrived, breathless with youthful excitement.

Chelsea's face broke into a happy smile, matching the brightness in her green eyes. "Guess what I made for you?'' she asked Jenna, keeping her surprise hidden behind her back.

Playing along for Chelsea's benefit, Jenna tapped her chin in thought. "Hmm. A quilt of daisies?"

Chelsea's laughter bubbled with joy. "Close." She presented her gift with a flourish. "Ta-da! It's a crown of flowers."

She'd meticulously wreathed the stems together to create a circlet of blossoms, that did, indeed, resemble a crown. Even Garrett was impressed with his daughter's artistic talent.

"I made it special for you," Chelsea said.

"Oh, sweetheart, it's beautiful." Misty, sentimental emotions shimmered in Jenna's eyes, and she pressed a hand to her chest, undeniably touched by Chelsea's gesture. "Will you do the honors and put it on me?"

"Sure." Stepping behind Jenna, Chelsea placed the coronet of flowers on her head, then came around to inspect her handiwork. "You look so pretty, Jenna. Just like a princess." Kneeling in front of them, Chelsea took Garrett's hand and folded it over Jenna's. "Daddy can be your prince, and we can all live happily ever after."

Jenna's breath caught at Chelsea's childish musings, reminding Garrett of something Jenna herself had said when he'd seen her that first night at Leisure Pointe. *I was supposed to marry a prince charming, and live happily ever after. I guess I'm just not very good at making wishes.*

Jenna managed a smile for Chelsea. "Yes, wouldn't that be nice," she said softly, though it was obvious to Garrett that she didn't believe such a fairy-tale ending was possible.

*   *   *

Jenna tiptoed quietly down the stairs, careful not to wake Ella Vee on her midnight trek to the kitchen. After this afternoon's conversation with Garrett on their picnic, she couldn't sleep, and decided that a decadent dessert was in order to soothe her troubled thoughts.

Retrieving a bowl and the vanilla ice cream, she helped herself to a generous scoop, and topped the treat with chocolate sauce. Taking her dessert to the table, she sat down, took a bite, and tried to sort through the worries and concerns plaguing her.

The gist of Garrett's "I don't want to hide the fact that you and I are seeing each other" comment meant he was ready to make their relationship public. While there was a particular safety and security in keeping their romance private, Jenna was now forced to make choices she'd avoided since arriving in Danby. Difficult choices she knew could change everything between her and Garrett—for the better, or worse, depended on *him*, and his reaction to her disgraceful past.

She swirled her spoon in her ice cream and took another bite. The risks in telling Garrett the truth were high, she knew. The fears she harbored were just as legitimate. She was keeping an integral part of her past from Garrett, and though her secret wasn't as devastating as his first wife's deceit, her dishonesty was just as misleading, with the potential to hurt him and his family if the information was ever brought out in the open by another source.

And then there was her own reputation to consider and the possibility of losing the respectability she'd gained because of Garrett, and the town's acceptance. She finally felt as though she belonged somewhere. A place where she was free to be her true self, without the kind of false pretenses her mother had tried to instill in her, or the kind of refined appearance Sheldon had needed to complete his image. Here in Danby she was just Jenna Phillips, proudly so, and the thought of giving up that sense of approval made her chest ache…as did the very real possibility of Garrett seeing her in a different light that no longer appealed to him once he discovered her secret.

So many regrets, so many risks…but Garrett had the right to know what she'd done, and why she'd posed for that lingerie catalog. He had the right to decide if he wanted to pursue a woman with such a disreputable past—a past that could never be erased or forgotten and would always be a part of *her*. He'd given her honesty and respect in their relationship, and he deserved it in return.

Because, ultimately, she'd fallen in love with Garrett Blackwell. With him, she wanted what her mother had searched a lifetime for, but had never been able to find for herself. Jenna yearned to be loved in return by one special man, wanted to be respected for who and what she was.

And in order for her and Garrett to have any kind of future together, she had to trust him with the truth. She had to trust in *him*, to understand her reasons, and not to judge her for something she'd *had* to do.

She took her empty bowl to the sink, rinsed it out, and drew a deep, fortifying breath. Now it was just a matter of finding the right time and place to bare her soul.

CHAPTER TEN

TONIGHT was the night, Jenna decided as she headed downstairs to wait for Garrett to arrive for their first official "date." She'd put off the inevitable conversation with Garrett long enough, much longer than she'd originally intended once she'd made the decision to tell him the truth about her past. There had been no opportune moment to bring up the subject during the week, and now, guilt was starting to settle on her conscience, and that was something she refused to allow to taint her growing relationship with Garrett.

Tonight *would* be the night, she vowed. Lisa had asked to take Chelsea for the night so her niece could spend some time with the twins, and Garrett wanted to take advantage of the evening alone to take Jenna out to dinner. While she didn't want to spoil their date with a discussion about her secret, before the evening was over, they needed to talk.

She entered the living room and smiled at Ella Vee as the older woman sat in her favorite overstuffed chair and worked on a floral cross-stitch pattern. She tipped her chin down to look at Jenna above the rim of her wire-framed glasses. "My, my," she said exuberantly. "Don't you look pretty."

"Thank you." Jenna smoothed a self-conscious hand over the bodice of the peach-colored dress she'd chosen to wear for tonight's intimate outing.

The outfit was made of a silky material that clung lightly to her breasts and waist, then flared over her hips and flirted around her knees in a way that show-cased her slender legs. She'd left her hair down and unrestrained, allowing the curls to cascade over her shoulders and back, just how Garrett liked it best. She wanted to look beautiful and feminine for him, wanted him to be proud to be seen with her.

She inwardly winced at her insecure thoughts. For all she'd grown in strength the past weeks, it was apparent she still possessed a bit of vulnerability she couldn't shake. But this night was so important to her, for so many reasons, and she'd be lying if she didn't admit that she was nervous.

Ella Vee rocked back in her chair. "Where are you off to on this fine Saturday night?"

"I'm going out to dinner with Garrett." Jenna glanced at her wristwatch, feeling both anxious and excited at the same time. "He should be here any minute."

"It's about time that boy took you out on the town," Ella Vee said with a satisfied nod. "He's been a little slow coming around, but I have a feeling he plays for keeps."

"I certainly hope so," she said softly, realizing too late that she'd spoken her thoughts aloud.

Ella Vee set aside her cross-stitch and regarded Jenna speculatively. "Things are serious between the two of you, aren't they?"

She sat down on the couch and shrugged indifferently, but couldn't stop the telltale warmth that infused her cheeks. "I enjoy being with him, and Chelsea." That was all she was willing to admit to Ella Vee, or anyone else for that matter, for now.

No one needed to know that both father and daughter had so thoroughly captured her heart, and in such a short span of time.

A knowing smile curved the corners of Ella Vee's mouth. "You have the same glow in your eyes that I felt for my beloved Byron when he first started courting me so many years ago." She pressed a hand to her chest and sighed. "Ah, to be young and in love again."

Startled by Ella Vee's observation, Jenna glanced away from the older woman's gaze, but couldn't deny feeling a bit giddy at the lovely notion of being courted. She'd never been romanced by any man, not even Sheldon. He'd pursued her for purely practical reasons, and that hadn't included frivolous dates and romantic interludes.

The doorbell rang, and Jenna's heart lurched in her chest.

Ella Vee smiled. "Looks like your man is here."

Her man. Jenna liked the sound of that. Taking a deep, relaxing breath, she pushed to her feet and went to answer the door. The man standing on the other side of the threshold took her breath away. She'd always thought Garrett gorgeous, but there was something about this whole entire night that made him seem like the prince of her dreams with his pitch-black hair and sexy blue eyes that appraised her outfit with as much interest as she took in his. His jeans and casual shirt were gone, replaced by a button-down shirt in brown tones and chocolate-colored trousers.

He held a fragrant bouquet of carnations and roses toward her. "These are for you."

A lump formed in her throat, making speech impossible. She took the floral arrangement, melting inside at the sweet gesture. "The flowers are beautiful, Garrett," she managed around the tightness in her chest. "Thank you."

"You're welcome." He grinned, making him look young, boyish, and carefree.

"Come on in," She stepped aside for him to enter the house. "I'm going to put these in water. I'll be just a minute."

Needing a quick reprieve to gather her composure, she headed toward the kitchen, listening as Garrett greeted Ella Vee. Finding a vase in the cupboard, she filled it with water and carefully arranged the flowers and baby's breath in the glass container.

She was so lost in her thoughts, she didn't hear him enter the kitchen. She gasped when he slipped his arms around her waist from behind and pulled her flush against his chest. Her entire body tingled at the contact.

"You look and smell good enough to eat," he growled into her ear, then buried his face into her hair to inhale a deep breath of her scent.

She shivered with pleasure and the stirring of desire taking up residence in her. Closing her eyes and reveling in every sensation he evoked, she reached back and placed her palm against his smooth cheek. "You look and smell pretty good yourself," she said.

His warm chuckle seemed to reverberate through her. "Aren't we a pair." He turned her in his arms, the irresistible heat glimmering in his eyes pure temptation. "We've got a full evening ahead of us. Ready to go?"

She nodded, willing to follow him anywhere.

* * *

The magical night ended much too soon for Jenna's liking.

Once they left Ella Vee's, Garrett treated her to dinner at the nicest restaurant in town, requesting a secluded booth and candlelight that gave the atmosphere a very intimate feel. While many people watched them with interest on their first public outing together, Garrett was openly attentive and affectionate. He touched her often, insisted on holding her hand, and refused to hide the fact that they were a couple.

He took her to a romantic comedy movie, and afterward they strolled along the closed shops, illuminated by the full moon and star-studded sky. He stopped to kiss her frequently, leaving her restless for more. And because Jenna was loathe to shatter the wondrous fantasy evening Garrett had woven, she couldn't bring herself to shift the romantic, playful mood to a more serious topic.

But just like Cinderella and her prince, the clock struck midnight, signaling that she'd avoided the inevitable much too long. Garrett ushered her back to his truck, slipped behind the wheel, and stretched his arm across the back of the bench seat toward her.

He brushed her loose hair aside and skimmed his fingers down her throat. "Do you want me to take you to the boarding house, or would you like to come back to my place for a while?" he asked, his deep voice as seductive as silk strumming along her skin. "I'm not expecting Rylan home tonight."

His insinuation was unmistakable. They'd be alone, cloaked in privacy. And that's exactly what she needed to divulge her secret, to tell him the truth about her past. Gathering the courage to put her future in Garrett's hands was another matter altogether.

"Your place," she whispered, and felt butterflies flutter in her tummy at the wholly masculine smile curving his mouth.

But when they arrived at his house, it was apparent that serious conversation wasn't anywhere on Garrett's agenda. He led her to the living room, keeping the lights dim, and the atmosphere romantic. A tantalizing shiver coursed through her, the sudden, unexpected chill suffusing her veins.

Garrett regarded her thoughtfully. "Would you like something to drink?" He rubbed his hands up and down her arms, warming her with his body heat. "Maybe a glass of wine?"

Grateful for his perception, she sat on the couch. "A glass of wine would be nice," she said, hoping that might calm the dozen insecurities that had taken flight within her and bolster the fortitude she so desperately needed to see her through the upcoming discussion.

He left her alone with her thoughts, but returned minutes later, giving her very little time to formulate an easy way to bring up what was on her mind. He handed her the glass of blush liquid, and settled in beside her—close enough that their thighs touched, and his enticing male scent saturated her senses with a familiar longing she tried hard to resist.

He wove his finger through a curly strand of her hair and gave it a gentle tug to capture her attention. "Ah, alone at last."

His dark, intense gaze captured hers in the golden lamplight, and she smiled. "Do you think Chelsea is having a good time with the twins?'' She took a long swallow of the wine, and it settled in her belly, warm and relaxing.

"I'm sure she's having a ball helping Lisa. She was so excited about spending the night and being with the twins.'' A grin touched his mouth, and he brushed his fingers along her jaw, igniting a very pleasurable sensation just beneath the surface of her skin. "You know, I've been wanting to thank you for everything you've done for Chelsea, too.''

She laughed lightly, trying to ignore the flicker of awareness his caress evoked. She had a mission to fulfill tonight, and couldn't afford to be distracted. "I haven't done much at all. I enjoy spending time with her.'' She took another drink of her wine, re-alizing she'd nearly drained the glass.

"Chelsea has really taken to you, not that I'm surprised, and so have I.'' Taking the wineglass from her, he set it on the coffee table in front of them. When he returned to her side, he swept her wild fall of curls aside, exposing her neck. He dipped his head and nuzzled the sensitive spot just below her ear. "I was thinking, once Lisa returns to the office, maybe you'd like to continue watching Chelsea? I'd keep your salary the same, of course, but I don't want you to think that's the only reason I'm making the offer.''

She closed her eyes as his lips set her flesh on fire, and managed a breathy, "Oh?''

His damp mouth opened against her throat, and he slid a hand down her spine, crushing her breasts against his chest. A moan rumbled in his throat. "I like having you here to come home to in the afternoons and evenings," he said, the tenor of his voice turning husky.

Her heart beat wildly as heat and need threatened to swamp her. She had to tell Garrett the truth, before he dragged her into the flames he was creating. Her doubts and fears returned in a rush of anxiety that shook her to the core.

He lifted his head, his expression infinitely tender and caring. "You're trembling, Jenna. Are you nervous?" he asked, his voice low and soothing.

Was he that in-tune to her? Or was she that transparent? "Yes. A little," she whispered. But for reasons he didn't yet understand.

A concerned frown creased his brows. "Do *I* make you nervous?"

She swallowed the knot of emotion gathering in her throat. Needing to touch him, she smoothed back the dark lock of hair that had fallen so rakishly over his forehead. "No, *you* don't make me nervous." *I'm just so scared of losing you once you discover what I've done.*

He caught her hand and pressed a kiss in her palm. "Then how do I make you feel?"

The answer to his question came easily. "Safe. Secure. Desirable." *Respectable.* And she feared losing that, too.

His smile was lazy and very sexy. "I'm glad I make you feel that way." Reclining against the end of the couch, he pulled her closer, and she flowed into his arms willingly. "Do you realize I haven't had you alone and all to myself in two days? I feel like I'm starting to go through symptoms of withdrawal."

Her mouth was positioned just above his, so near

she could almost taste his kiss. She dragged her tongue along her bottom lip. "Are you suggesting that you have lost time to make up for?"

His hand slipped to the nape of her neck, his wonderful fingers gently kneading the tense muscles there, making her feel lethargic. "Maybe I do," he murmured.

Her breath left her lungs in a rush. Temptation beckoned, pulling her in two distinctly different directions. Her body softened, grew pliant, while her mind urged her to pull away and put much needed distance between them. She fought her way through the sensual fog settling over her, just barely.

"Garrett—"

"No more talking, Jenna." He effectively cut her off with his words, and the slow exploration of his hands along her waist and over her bottom. Slowly, he inched up the hem of her dress, until his palms encountered the backs of her bare thighs.

She gasped, and a sexy grin lifted his lips.

"We talked all evening. Now it's just you and me, and I have a different form of communication in mind."

His eyes turned a smoldering shade of blue, and she wanted nothing more than to lose herself in his gaze and never be found again. There was so much about this man she *did* want...she yearned to touch him everywhere, ached to hold him close and feel his body against hers—heartbeat to heartbeat.

More than anything, she longed for his love.

For now, for the moment, she'd settle for desire and passion. Her lashes fluttered to half-mast. "One kiss," she relented as he drew her mouth to his and she surrendered to him.

But Garrett was like a potent, addictive drug, and one taste wasn't nearly enough to satisfy her hunger. He slanted his mouth beneath hers as each kiss melted inevitably, enticingly into another, until the only thought filling her head, the only emotion in her heart, was being one with this man who'd made her feel so whole and complete.

Before she changed her mind, before she allowed her better judgment to intrude on the sensual moment, she whispered her greatest need against his lips, "Garrett, make love to me."

He stilled, the muscles across his chest bunching. "Are you sure?"

She'd never been more sure of anything in her entire life, and she supposed love had a way of turning doubts into certainties. Selfish as it might be, she wanted this one night with Garrett, wanted to meld her heart with his, and let their souls entwine in a way she'd never before experienced. "Yes, I'm sure."

He stared at her for a long moment, his eyes searching hers. "No regrets in the morning?"

She shook her head, knowing the only thing she'd ever regret was not making love with him. It would be a beautiful memory she'd forever cherish, no matter what tomorrow, and the truth, would bring. "No regrets."

With that solemn promise, he led her up the stairs to his bedroom, where there were no more lengthy conversations to worry about, just the anticipation of pleasure. Instead of words, they communicated with their lips, their hands, and their bodies.

Standing by the big four-poster she'd slept alone in weeks earlier as they slowly, leisurely undressed each other, Jenna realized that she'd come full circle. From a runaway bride seeking a place where she belonged, to a woman who'd found all that, and so much more. And tonight, she refused to allow her past to overshadow this moment of pure contentment, and the bliss awaiting her.

With each article of clothing Garrett stripped away, he caressed the flesh he'd bared, and she reveled in the exquisite sensations tumbling through her. And then she helped him shed his own clothes, and was struck by the sheer physical beauty of his body, the strength of his desire for her, as well as her own feminine reaction to him. She experienced no apprehension with him. No shame. Just a rightness that filled her to overflowing.

He pulled down the covers and eased her back onto the mattress, and after taking a moment for protection, he covered her with his hard length, finding his natural place between her legs. While she automatically braced herself for this first joining, it seemed Garrett was in no rush to complete the union. While one hand delved into her hair, his other skimmed her body with need, warmth, and an urgency that left her breathless. His kisses were deep and reverent, and he completely seduced her mouth before his lips left hers to blaze a trail down her throat to her full, taut breasts. She shivered at the erotic brush of his breath against her skin, and the excitement coiling tight in her belly.

He lifted his head just as he reached the tip of her breast, his gaze rich with appreciation as he took in her lush figure. "Ah, Jenna, you're absolutely perfect, so incredibly beautiful," he whispered. He curved his hand possessively around her soft, feminine flesh and skimmed his thumb over the hard peak.

She inhaled a startled breath, stunned by the intense ache spreading within her. "Thank you," she said, her tone shy, matching the blush she knew was staining her cheeks.

He studied her face, surprise lighting his eyes. "No man has ever told you that before?"

His incredulous tone made her smile. The shift of his legs along hers created sparks she felt from her head all the way to her toes. "You're the first."

"Amazing," he murmured, and dipped his head to lavish attention on the breasts he'd just praised.

The heat of his mouth, the softness of his tongue, all conspired to make her wild and restless with sensual longing and something far more pleasurable. Moaning softly, she pushed her fingers through his thick hair, and clung to him. She'd never felt so cherished, so utterly worshiped, and it was a feeling she never wanted to end.

Unable to help herself, she touched him in return, running her hands over his hard muscles, down his arms and over his chest, until he was just as feverish as she.

And then his lips crushed hers in a rapacious kiss and she felt the pressure of him pushing against her. She gasped sharply at the invasion, and the twinge of pain she experienced at being stretched too quickly. But the discomfort ebbed as he moved, filling her completely, building the pleasure until they were both swept into the awaiting storm. Just as Jenna wished, she felt connected not only by their bodies, but their hearts and souls as well.

The emotions that crashed over her in the aftermath overwhelmed her. Her breath caught on an unexpected shudder, and tears of happiness filled her eyes.

Garrett lifted his head from the crook of her neck, and frowned when he saw the moisture shimmering in her eyes. One blink, and a tear escaped, and he brushed it away with his thumb.

Concern etched his bold, masculine features. "Jenna, honey, are you all right?"

"I'm fine." She pressed her palm to his cheek and gave him a reassuring smile. "I just never knew making love would be this perfect."

Understanding dawned in slow degrees, infusing his velvet blue eyes with shock. "You're a virgin?"

"Not anymore," she whispered.

Braced on his forearm, Garrett couldn't take his gaze off the satiated woman laying beside him on his bed. The lamplight illuminated her incredible body flushed with luxurious fulfillment, her wild curly hair spread over his pillow, and her soft mouth. But despite that enticing visual display, it was Jenna's eyes that held him riveted. The depths reflected a vulnerability that wrapped around his heart and made him feel extremely protective of her.

He supposed being her first lover had something to do with his fierce feelings as well. And that particular revelation still baffled him—that this very sensual woman had saved herself...for him.

The gift humbled him, pleased him, and brought too many questions rushing to the surface of his mind. He expressed the most predominant one. "Jenna, why didn't you tell me you've never been with another man?" *Not even her fiancé.*

She tugged the sheet up, covering her breasts, and turned more fully toward him, so they were face-to-face. "It never came up in conversation."

Her tone held a teasing lilt, but her simple answer didn't satisfy him. "You can do better than that, sweetheart." His knuckles drifted down her soft cheek, over that enticing beauty mark near her mouth, then across her bare shoulder. "You had plenty of opportunities to say something, like *before* we came upstairs."

She placed a hand on his chest, right over where his heart beat steadily, while her eyes held his captive. "Garrett...I didn't want it to matter."

But her being a virgin *did* matter, for so many different reasons. He'd taken something from her he could never give back, despite the fact that she'd freely given herself to *him.* "How come you've never been with another man?" he asked, curious to know the reasons she'd resisted such a natural progression to any serious relationship. "Not even Sheldon."

"No, not even Sheldon," she agreed softly as she absently traced a pattern on his chest with her finger. "After everything my mother had been through with men, most of whom used her and took advantage of her, she preached the importance of being respected *and* respectable when I started developing breasts and other curves. She didn't want anyone taking advantage of me, and believed being respected by a man was much more important than love, because that emotion made a person weak. My mother truly loved my father, and he broke her heart. She was never the same after that and felt as though she lost both love and her respectability. It's been a lifelong lesson for me.''

He suspected there was more to that lifelong lesson. For as much as she revealed, the sadness in her eyes hid so much more. ''Jenna, I have to ask...after saving yourself for this many years, and now knowing your reasons, why *me?*''

''Because you're a man of honor and integrity, and being with you feels right.'' She swallowed convulsively, and a tremulous smile wavered on her lips. ''And...I love you.''

For the second time that night, Jenna stunned him, rendering him speechless.

''Garrett, I don't expect you to say it in return,'' she rushed to assure him. ''I just wanted you to know that I don't take making love with you lightly.''

He believed her. While Angela had manipulated him for her own selfish gains, there was no denying that Jenna was nothing like his first wife. She had a pure heart and a giving spirit, which was exactly what drew him to her in ways he couldn't fight.

He lowered his head and kissed her, and she matched his desire on all levels. Exquisitely so. Primitive need gripped him, and he pulled her into his arms and gently eased her beneath his hard body, wanting her with an intensity that made him impatient and greedy.

She broke the kiss, her breath coming in short gasps as she seemingly struggled to keep from being swept away by their passion for each other. Her luminous eyes found his in the shadowed room. ''Garrett...we need to talk.''

He smiled down at her. ''We just did. You told

me all I need to know for tonight." He dropped a kiss on her nose, her cheek, her lips. "Tomorrow we have all day together, and we'll talk about anything you want." His hands stroked away any other protest she would have tried to make, and his persuasive mouth melted the last of her resistance, leaving her pliant and dewy with wanting.

And as Garrett made love to Jenna again, he accepted the realization that he'd fallen in love with her, too.

CHAPTER ELEVEN

MORNING came much too quickly for Jenna. After a wondrous night in Garrett's arms, it was difficult to face the reality of day...and the discussion she'd put off for too long. The direction of her future, the security of what lay in her heart, depended on Garrett and his reaction to her deepest, most locked-away secret.

With a sigh, she touched the empty pillow beside her where Garrett had slept. It was after nine in the morning, she was alone in his big bed, but she could hear him in the kitchen and smell the scents of breakfast. Her stomach rumbled hungrily, urging her to get up and join him downstairs.

But first she showered, used Garrett's toiletries to brush her teeth and hair, and changed back into the dress she'd worn the day before. And as she caught her reflection in the bathroom mirror, she saw subtle changes in herself, and realized that she glowed from not only their lovemaking, but love itself.

She'd taken a risk last night by declaring her feelings to Garrett, but he hadn't rejected her love. In fact, his actions gave her every reason to believe his emotions were just as intimately entwined with hers. She'd tasted his caring in his kiss, felt his tenderness in his touch, and had seen the warmth and devotion in his eyes when he'd made her his.

She'd found love and passion with a man. Now, she needed that same man's respect.

Heading downstairs, she entered the kitchen and let her gaze linger on Garrett as he stood at the stove scrambling eggs. He'd taken a shower, too. His damp hair brushed the collar of his casual knit shirt and faded jeans hugged his lean hips and long legs. He was simply a gorgeous man, and her reaction to him was exciting and breathtaking.

"Good morning," she said, coming up beside him. She caressed a hand down his back, needing to touch him, wanting to feel that same connection she had last night. And she needed to know that in the light of day, nothing between them had changed.

He grinned at her, his eyes a deep, velvet shade of blue. "Hey, I was wondering when you were going to get up." He dipped his head and gave her a quick but meaningful kiss. An undeniable stamp of possession she didn't mind in the least.

Her lips tingled with pleasure. "Um, I don't normally sleep in this late." She picked up a piece of crisp bacon and took a bite. "I have a certain someone to blame for a sleepless night."

He scooped the fluffy eggs onto two plates, then turned off the burner. "If you're looking for an apology, honey, you're not going to get one, because I didn't hear that mouth of yours complain that I was keeping you awake. Not even once."

Impossible as it seemed after last night and all they'd shared, she felt a blush tinge her cheeks. "True."

He merely laughed, the sound husky and warm and very intimate. "Are you hungry?"

"As a matter of fact, I'm starved."

After helping him set the table, they sat down to the bacon and eggs he'd made, and orange juice.

The food was delicious and filling, and their conversation was light and easy, setting a comfortable mood Jenna planned to use to her advantage once breakfast was over.

Together, they did the dishes, and just as Jenna was drying off her hands and trying to figure out the best opening, Garrett slipped up behind her, wrapped his arms around her waist, and buried his face in her unbound hair. Closing her eyes, she leaned into him, absorbing his strength.

Very casually, and with little effort, he maneuvered her out of the kitchen and into the living room, then stopped before going further. He met her gaze, the depths of his glinting with a wickedly sensual light. "What do you say you and I head back upstairs and take advantage of being alone just a little while longer?"

His suggestion sounded wonderful, and so tempting. She hated to spoil the closeness between them, the romantic feelings, and refusing him wasn't easy. "Your sister is going to bring Chelsea back soon, and there's no telling when Rylan will come home, either."

"You're right." A disappointed sigh escaped him, accompanied by a gracious smile. "But you can't blame me for trying."

She slipped from his arms, and instantly missed his supportive embrace. "Garrett, there's something I need to tell you."

He tipped his head, his playful mood turning into concern. "Sounds serious."

"It could be." She crossed her arms over her chest, not surprised at the reappearance of yesterday's nerves. "It's about what happened on my wedding day, and the reason why I couldn't marry Sheldon.''

He paused for a moment, then, ''I've been waiting for this.''

His admission startled her. ''You have?''

His broad shoulders lifted in a shrug. ''I've suspected that there was more than just a compatibility issue between you and Sheldon.''

She frowned, wondering where and how he'd come to that conclusion. ''What made you think there was something more?''

''That first night in the bar, you looked so lost and alone,'' he said gently. ''And you mentioned that you'd humiliated Sheldon and his family, though I can't imagine for the life of me you doing anything so awful.''

Oh, but she had!

The sound of a vehicle pulling up to the front of the house diverted their attention. Garrett glanced out the window and sighed. ''Looks like Chelsea's home.''

Jenna wanted to wail in frustration at yet another delay. A sense of urgency and desperation filled her. ''Garrett, we *have* to talk.''

''And we will. Later.'' He came back to her, wrapping her in a brief, but comforting hug, and placed a kiss on her cheek. ''I promise.''

She held tight to that assurance, and a minute later Chelsea and Lisa came through the front door, with Duane following behind toting two separate carriers for the babies.

''Jenna, Dad, guess what!'' Chelsea said as she raced into the house. ''Aunt Lisa let me hold Jacob and Janet, and I even got to feed them and put powder on their bottoms when Aunt Lisa changed their diapers!''

Jenna laughed. "That sounds like fun." She peeked in on one of the twins—Janet, judging by the pink romper she was wearing—and tickled her fingers on the infant's tummy. Janet scrunched up her face and made a squeaking sound. "They're absolutely precious."

"When they're sleeping," Lisa said wryly.

The lines of exhaustion beneath the other woman's eyes were unmistakable. "Hopefully they'll settle into a routine soon."

Lisa unstrapped Janet from her carrier, and automatically handed the squirming infant to Jenna, then retrieved Jacob. "They're getting better about sleeping for longer stretches of time, but I'm looking forward to when they sleep through the entire night."

While the women fussed over the twins, Garrett headed outside to shoot the breeze with Duane on the front porch. Once they were gone and Jenna and Lisa were situated on the couch with the babies, Lisa cast a knowing glance Jenna's way.

"It's nice to see you and Garrett together," she said, handing a pacifier to Jenna for the baby. "It's been a long time since he's let a woman into his life, and you've been good for him."

Jenna absorbed the other woman's words as she gently rocked baby Janet in her arms. "He's been good for me, too." In ways that had altered her life for the better. In ways that would change her future and hopefully give her the kind of contentment she felt at this very moment.

*   *   *

So much for wishing he and Jenna could spend Sunday morning alone, Garrett thought as he sat out on the front porch, conversing casually with Duane about an electrical job he'd recently acquired. Not only had his sister and brother-in-law interrupted them with their early arrival, but Rylan was now home, too.

Garrett watched his brother step out of his truck and approach the house without his normal carefree exuberance. In fact, Rylan looked downright grim as he climbed the porch stairs.

"What's the matter, Ry?" Garrett grinned lazily. "Did Emma kick you out of her bed too early this morning?"

"No, Emma and I are just fine." Rylan glanced from Duane, back to Garrett, his expression turning resigned. "I've got something I think you need to see." He extended the magazine he held in his hand.

Garrett promptly frowned as he read the familiar *Barely There* title on the glossy cover and took in the picture of a woman dressed in a very head-turning negligee. Duane looked on with interest, too.

"What's this?" Obvious confusion tinged Garrett's voice.

Rylan hesitated for a brief moment, as if reconsidering his response. "It's a lingerie catalog that Beau was passing around at Leisure Pointe last night."

Just the mention of the man who'd harassed Jenna made Garrett's hackles rise. "And?" he prompted his brother, sensing there was more.

Rylan sighed, the sound rife with regret. "Jenna's in there."

Garrett shook his head, certain he'd misheard his brother. "What?"

"Jenna posed for the catalog, Garrett, in some pretty sexy stuff," Rylan said bluntly, and shoved the magazine into his hands, forcing him to acknowledge what he was saying. "And Beau made sure that everyone got a good look at her, too."

Garrett didn't want to believe Rylan, didn't want to believe that Jenna could keep something like this from him. Unable to help himself, and out of morbid curiosity, Garrett flipped through the pages. Sure enough, there was Jenna, in sultry poses, wearing sensual, provocative lingerie, and looking more like a centerfold sex kitten than the wholesome, guileless woman he'd allowed into his home and bed, and held in his arms last night.

A woman he didn't really know at all, he realized.

His stomach churned, reminding him of another woman's betrayal, and the turmoil she'd put his life through—he felt trapped and duped, in much the same way as he had when Angela manipulated him.

Brooding anger made his jaw clench. "How... where did Beau get this?"

"I assumed you'd want to know that, and *persuaded* Beau to give me that answer," Rylan replied, leaving no doubt in Garrett's mind that his brother had resorted to strong-arm tactics to gain the information. "He said he was with some woman Friday night, and found the catalog at her place, laying on her coffee table and he started glancing through the pages..."

Garrett held up a hand to stop him, following the gist of where Rylan was heading with his comment.

"You didn't know," Rylan said flatly, knowingly. "She didn't tell you."

"No." But now he knew what Jenna had tried to

tell him last night, and again this morning. But he'd had a right to know about her past, *before* he'd made love to her. *Before* he'd allowed her closer than any other woman. And it irked him that she hadn't trusted him enough to tell him the truth long before last night.

Now he couldn't help but wonder if she'd slept with him with ulterior motives in mind, if in giving him her innocence she now expected him to do the chivalrous thing and marry her...to keep her "respectable" and cover up her scandalous past.

He snorted at that, feeling like a fool. *Again.*

"I'm sorry, Garrett," Rylan said, placing a compassionate hand on his shoulder. "But if I didn't tell you, you'd hear it from someone else. Everybody's talking about the catalog and Jenna. And you. Emma agreed that I should just show this to you and get it over with."

He appreciated his brother's loyalty, but he found it difficult to accept Jenna's duplicity, not when they'd never had the kind of honesty he demanded in a relationship. And it made him furious to realize that the town knew about Jenna's side job as a lingerie model before he did. No doubt, within a matter of days gossip would surround him and his family.

He swore beneath his breath and stood. "If you two will excuse me, I think Jenna and I have something we need to discuss." His voice was calm, despite the tension stringing his muscles tight.

Curling the catalog into his hand, he headed back inside the house and stopped short at the sight of Jenna cooing so sweetly to one of the babies, her face soft and achingly beautiful. She glanced up when the screen door slammed shut, and smiled at him in a way that made him feel broad-sided. In a way that made him wish he wasn't holding damning, compelling evidence against her in the palm of his hand.

"Jenna, can I talk to you? Privately?"

The undisguised bite in his voice caused his sister to slant him a curious look, and even garnered Chelsea's attention. Jenna looked at first startled by his clipped tone, then worried. She set the baby she was holding into Chelsea's lap, and in silence followed him upstairs to his bedroom. She'd made the bed before coming downstairs earlier, but it wasn't difficult for Garrett to recall how soft, warm, and willing she'd been with him last night. That memory would haunt him forever, he was certain—like every night when he lay in that bed. Alone.

He didn't waste time confronting her. The sooner they got this unpleasant discussion over with, the sooner she could be on her way. And he was fairly certain this very public revelation would prompt her to leave Danby, and move on to somewhere new.

He let the catalog unfurl for her to see. "Care to explain this?"

She inhaled a sharp breath. Her hand fluttered to her chest, and her gaze jerked from the *Barely There* cover, to him. But she didn't deny the truth staring up at her. "Garrett...*that* is what I tried to talk to you about earlier."

"Don't you think this is something I deserved to know about *before* we made love?" Not giving her a chance to answer, he flipped to a page previewing her wearing a low-cut, very short and filmy baby-doll nightie that displayed more curves than it covered. "It would have been nice to know ahead of time that the woman I was seeing had posed for a risqué lingerie spread for *everyone* to see." Indignation laced his voice.

She visibly winced, and her cheeks turned a bright shade of pink. He found it difficult to believe that she could blush so guilelessly after posing for these seductive pictures. He felt torn between holding on to the generous, sweet woman he'd made love to last night, and pushing away the woman she'd been before he'd ever met her. He had no idea who the real Jenna was.

"You're right," she whispered in agreement, her voice sounding strangled by emotion. But amazingly, she held her head high. "I should have told you weeks ago about the catalog, and I'm sorry that you had to find out this way. I never meant for any of this to hurt you, or your family."

She didn't break down and cry as he'd expected. She didn't beg for his forgiveness, and she didn't apologize for what she'd done in her past, just for hurting *him*. He clenched his jaw, and shored up his defenses, refusing to allow himself to soften so easily. Not when he had firsthand experience of just how manipulative some women could be for their own gain and purposes.

"I'm sure this will start a nice little scandal here in Danby, and the last thing I want or need after Angela is a woman with these kinds of surprises lurking in her past. I don't need the speculation focused on me or my family."

He tossed the catalog onto the bed, and the circular magazine ironically opened to a page with Jenna wearing a silky camisole and matching tap pants. "Why didn't you tell me sooner, Jenna?"

She laughed dryly, but her eyes held no humor. "I've never told *anyone*, Garrett. That lingerie spread isn't something I'm exactly proud of."

He stared at her for a long moment. "Then why did you do it?"

"At the time, I had no choice." Jenna hated the disapproval so evident in the taut line of his body, in the darkening of his eyes. It was exactly the reaction she'd feared, yet she couldn't fault him for being upset and angry with her. All she could do was attempt to explain her actions.

"When my mother died, the medical bills she'd accumulated from her emphysema became mine. I had no way of paying them off, and I took the modeling job to earn extra money. I did a few lingerie layouts, knowing they could turn up in future catalogs, but at the time all I could think of was getting myself out of debt." And she'd sacrificed her respectability for that money, and she was fairly certain it had cost her true love, too.

He said nothing, just watched her, his mouth thinned with displeasure. Cold seeped into her veins, stealing the warmth she'd known for only a brief time with Garrett.

Drawing a deep, stabilizing breath, she continued, wanting him to know everything. "That was about a year before I met Sheldon, and I thought it was a part of the past, and something that was done and forgotten. My decision to marry Sheldon, and his to marry me, was based more on practical reasons, as you know. He wanted a decorous wife, and I wanted the kind of respectability my mother always insisted was of the utmost importance in a relationship."

Her mother had been right about one thing—love

did; indeed, come with heartache. At the moment, the pain was so profound it took all her strength to keep from giving in to the horrible pressure in her chest and the sting of emotion behind her eyes. Later, in private, she'd indulge in the grief of losing Garrett, the one man she'd believed would understand the choices she'd made. And maybe he would have—if she'd trusted him with the truth much, much sooner. If she hadn't let her fears get in the way of doing the right thing.

"What happened on your wedding day, Jenna?" he asked, his tone gruff and distant, but undeniably curious.

She sat on the edge of the bed and cast a glance at the picture of herself—so long ago, yet she could remember the photo shoot as if it were yesterday. "An old, jilted girlfriend of Sheldon's came across the catalog, and just as the ceremony began, she walked in to the church, interrupted the minister, and presented my layout to the congregation. I was horrified, as was his family, considering the scandal and uproar that caused. I was ashamed and humiliated, and I did the only thing I could think of...I ran, but it's apparent that I'll never be able to run far enough."

Closing the catalog, she pushed it away, and forced herself to meet Garrett's penetrating gaze. "In a way, Sheldon's ex-girlfriend did both of us a favor. It would have been a mistake to marry him, I realize that now," she said softly. Now she knew what love was, and she refused to settle for less. "I would have been miserable, and so would Sheldon."

He folded his arms over his wide chest, his stance

stiff and unyielding. "And where do I fit in all this?"

Her stomach cramped with an awful foreboding. "What do you mean?"

"After last night, do you expect me to marry you to keep your respectability intact?" Bitterness coated his words and glimmered in his eyes.

His words struck her like a physical blow, his meaning very clear. She'd given him her virginity, and he believed she'd done so in an attempt to dupe him—as Angela had years ago.

Any hope she might have harbored for his forgiveness withered in that moment. She stood, gathering the tattered shreds of her dignity. "You don't owe me anything, Garrett. Nothing at all." She'd never take something from him that he wasn't willing to offer freely. "I'll have Lisa take me home."

She crossed the room to the closed door, wishing he'd call out for her to stay so they could talk out this problem, but his silence made it very clear that he wanted her gone. For him, there was nothing left to discuss.

But before she walked out of his life, there was something she wanted to say to him, and needed him to hear. Hand on the doorknob, she stopped and glanced back, praying her brave composure held on for just a few seconds longer. "Garrett, I know you're not sure what to believe right now, but there is one truth in all of this. I meant what I said last night when I told you that I loved you."

His expression remained impassive, unreadable, and Jenna realized she'd lost Garrett before she ever truly had him. All because of a past mistake *she* hadn't been able to come to terms with on her own.

After all, how could she expect him to accept her past and the choices she'd made when she hadn't been able to reconcile it for herself?

Garrett blew out a frustrated sigh and scrubbed a hand down his face, unable to concentrate on the work spread out on his desk in front of him. It had been almost a week since he'd let Jenna walk out of his house, out of his life, and he hadn't seen or heard from her since. A painful week of gossip and speculation surrounding Jenna's lingerie layout, and his relationship with her.

Jenna's *Barely There* spread had been a hot topic, one that had spread fast and furiously, and had died quicker than Garrett would have expected. A few days, to be exact. Once the novelty and shock of Jenna's scandalous past had worn off, everything settled back to normal.

Everything except Garrett's life. Nothing had been the same since he'd let her go. Not Chelsea. Not his empty, quiet office. And especially not his heart.

"How long do you plan to mope around?"

Garrett glared at his brother as Rylan sauntered into his office after a day working out in the field. "I don't mope," he said succinctly.

"You never used to," Rylan agreed with a light-hearted grin. "But not only do you look downright miserable, you've been too damned moody since your split with Jenna. Whatever happened to kissing and making up?"

He pushed a contract aside and grunted at his brother's easy cure-all. "What Jenna kept from me isn't as easily forgiven as that."

"I agree what she did was wrong, and she should have told you the truth right up front." Rylan sighed and pushed his fingers through his tousled hair. "I know I was the bearer of bad news, so to speak, but haven't *you* ever made a mistake that you've regretted later?" The obvious question didn't require an answer. "She's still around, Garrett, and it's not too late. She could be everything you need, if you just let her. And if you can't bring yourself to forgive her, then at least try and establish some kind of cordial relationship with her so it's not so awkward for the rest of the family." With that piece of advice, his brother left the office.

Garrett slumped back into his seat, feeling both frustrated and uncertain. He knew running into Jenna was inevitable, especially since she'd remained in Danby. That in itself surprised him, when he'd fully expected her to move on to escape the gossip. Maybe he did need to confront the issue, and Jenna one last time so they could both put this unpleasantness behind them and go their separate ways.

He wrapped things up early at the office, and on his way to pick up Chelsea decided to stop by Ella Vee's. The older woman greeted him at the door when he knocked and invited him inside.

Ella Vee's gaze swept over him from head to toe in a mildly chastising way. "I take it you're here to see Jenna?"

He ducked his head, feeling sheepish and not certain how she'd managed to provoke such a response. "Yes, ma'am, I am."

"It's about time," she muttered beneath her breath, just loud enough for Garrett to hear. Then

she hooked a finger toward the rear of the house.
"She's out in the backyard."

Heading in that direction, he crossed through the
kitchen and came to an abrupt stop at the window
overlooking the backyard. He caught sight of Jenna
outside, kneeling on the grass as she planted a flat
of pansies in the soft soil edging the yard.

He expected a renewed rush of anger upon seeing
her after being deceived and lied to, but instead experienced a deep yearning ache that told him he'd
forgiven Jenna long before this moment of reckon-
ing. He'd just been way too stubborn to admit it, his
pride too bruised to see past his own personal turmoil and confusion to resolve his true feelings for
Jenna.

He stood there, hands braced on the counter,
watching her for long silent moments. It wasn't so
much what she'd done by posing for that lingerie
spread, but that she hadn't trusted him with the truth
before he'd allowed his emotions to get involved
with her.

He'd initially felt betrayed and manipulated by
the secret she'd hid from him, but there was one fact
that pushed its way to the front of his mind. Despite
Jenna's past, there was no denying he would have
fallen for her, anyway. Her only fault had been in
waiting to tell him the truth, and he'd unjustly pun-
ished her for the mistake she'd made. Her silence
had been based on insecurities and fears he now
understood.

Regret banded his chest, along with more powerful emotions he could no longer deny. How could
he expect Jenna to have faith in him when he'd
given her no reason to believe he'd accept a past

she could never erase? She probably thought he was no better than Sheldon for letting her go, for giving her every reason to think that his reputation was far more important to him than taking a risk on the honest, guileless woman she truly was.

A passionate woman who loved him, despite the way he'd silently rejected that love. A beautiful woman who'd make him a perfect, respectable wife...if she'd forgive *him* for unfairly judging her.

Knowing he had to try and make amends, he headed outside and approached where she was tending to the flowers she planted. Sunshine haloed her in a warm, golden glow, and despite the painful ordeal she'd been through the past few days, there was an aura of peaceful contentment surrounding her that drew him. And as he closed the distance between them, he found himself awed by just how courageous and strong she'd been to remain in a town where everyone now knew of the catalog, to stay and face her biggest fear when it would have been so much easier for her to leave and avoid rumors and speculation.

She was amazing, and he respected the determination and fortitude that she'd found within herself. Without a shadow of a doubt, he respected *her*.

He stopped just behind her, casting a shadow over her kneeling figure. She glanced over her shoulder with a smile that ebbed into surprise when she met his gaze.

"Garrett," she said, her voice breathless and uncertain.

"Hello, Jenna." His voice was low, and incredibly calm, despite the rapid beating of his heart. "How are you?"

"I'm...okay." She stood, pulled off her gardening gloves, and brushed at the dirt caked on her knees.

Garrett's gaze lingered on her legs, then slowly drew upward to her face when she finally straightened. "Can I talk to you?"

Caution etched her features, and for a moment he thought she'd say no, not that he would have been able to blame her after the way he'd treated her the last time they'd been together.

"Sure," she said, prompting a polite smile. "Do you mind if we go to the back porch? I've been out in the sun for a few hours and I'm starting to feel light-headed."

With a nod, he escorted her to the shade of the porch and sat across from her at the picnic-style table. Her face was flushed from the warmth of the summer day, and a light sheen of perspiration dotted her brow. Her eyes were a bright shade of periwinkle, but it was the reserve he suddenly detected that made him more than a little nervous and made him wonder if he'd waited too long to finally come to his senses. The thought of having lost Jenna for good made his stomach wrench unbearably.

She stared at him expectantly, waiting for him to say whatever was on his mind. He cleared his throat and said, "I expected you to leave Danby after your *Barely There* debut," he said, injecting a bit of dry humor into his voice.

Her expression remained completely serious. "I considered it," she admitted.

"And what stopped you?" he asked, needing to know her reasons for staying.

"I came to the conclusion that I can't escape my

past and what I've done every time that lingerie catalog might surface somewhere.'' She hesitated a heartbeat, then a tremulous smile eased across her lips. ''And I realized that if I left, it would only fuel the gossip around here and tarnish what we shared, and that's something I refuse to allow to happen.''

Garrett was momentarily stunned by what she'd so selflessly done for him, for *them,* as well as the depth of her devotion and feelings.

''I can't let my past dictate my future or my own personal happiness any longer,'' she went on before he could get a word in edgewise. ''My mother always preached respectability, but I've come to realize that in order to be respectable, I had to respect myself first. And I do. This is who I am, Garrett, flaws and mistakes and everything else, and I'm hoping that everyone here in Danby will accept me for Jenna the person, not Jenna the lingerie model.''

And judging by how quickly the gossip had died, it seemed Jenna was well on her way to accomplishing that goal. ''I owe you an apology, Jenna.''

She frowned. ''What for?''

Reaching across the table, he settled his hand over hers. He felt her start at the unexpected touch, but didn't sever the connection he needed so badly. ''I was wrong for believing that your reasons for keeping your past a secret were anything but pure, and your way of protecting me and Chelsea from harmful gossip.''

She bit her bottom lip, and her eyes shimmered with moisture. ''You really do understand. I never meant to hurt anyone.''

He nodded. ''I know that now.''

Slowly, she lifted the hand beneath his so that

their fingers slid together and intertwined. Her eyes never left his. "I never intentionally set out to deceive you, Garrett. Keeping my past concealed was borne of self-preservation, much in the same way you keep your own secret of your daughter's parentage from Chelsea, to protect yourself as much as her."

He understood the comparison, and agreed. He swallowed back the lump that had formed in his throat. "I've let what happened with Angela blind me to just how good a relationship could be with the right woman. With *you*."

"I can't change the past, Garrett," she whispered in an emotion-filled voice, one that begged him to accept something that would forever be a part of her.

"I can't change my past, either, so I guess that makes us even." He smiled, feeling more optimistic than he had in days. "We all have regrets and things we'd do differently given the chance. If I had the ability to turn back the clock, I never would have let you walk out of my life the other day. All we can do is accept our mistakes and move forward. And my biggest mistake was not believing in your love."

"I do love you," she said, her eyes shining with the declaration. "More than I thought it possible to love another person."

"And I love you, too." Standing, he came around to her side of the table and pulled her up until she was standing in front of him, so very close their bodies brushed. "I'm hoping like hell I can repair our relationship and any damage I might have done to your heart."

She pressed her palm to his cheek. "You already have."

"You fill my life with laughter and love, Jenna, and I want you to come home with me, where you belong. I want to make a respectable woman out of you. That is, if you'll have me for better or worse."

Her eyes widened in shock, then quickly filled with overwhelming joy. "Oh, Garrett!" Wrapping her arms around his neck, she hugged him tight. Then her sweet, heavenly mouth found his, and the desire and promise Garret tasted in her kiss made him groan in satisfaction and pleasure.

Too soon the intimate moment ended and Jenna pulled back.

Fortunately the arm he'd banded around her waist kept her intimately close. He wasn't about to let her go, not until he knew for certain she was truly and completely his.

"You never did answer my question, sweetheart," he said, staring deeply into her eyes, so deep he thought he was drowning in pure adoration. "Are you gonna say yes and make me and Chelsea incredibly happy? Will you marry me and be my wife?"

This time, she didn't hesitate. "Yes, Garrett Blackwell, I'll marry you and be your wife."

And in that blissful, breathtaking instant, all of Jenna's wishes came true.

EPILOGUE

LESS than a year later, on a beautiful spring afternoon, Jenna married her prince charming. With Lisa as her matron-of-honor and Chelsea as her flower girl, Jenna vowed to love, honor and cherish Garrett, and he promised to do the same.

The minister pronounced them husband and wife and introduced them to the congregation as Mr. and Mrs. Garrett Blackwell. Jenna met her husband's dark eyes, saw the tender smile he gave her, and a sense of belonging filled her to overflowing. Garrett had found himself a bride on that long ago night at Leisure Pointe, but she'd gained so much more.

In that perfect moment of joy, she put her past behind her and stepped with her prince into a bright and glorious future filled with respect, love, and her very own happily-ever-after.

What happens when you suddenly
discover your happy twosome is about
to turn into a...*family?*
Do you laugh?
Do you cry?
Or...do you get married?

The answer is all of the above—and plenty more!

Share the laughter and tears with
Harlequin Romance® as these
unsuspecting couples have to be

READY FOR BABY

When parenthood takes you by surprise!

Authors to look out for include:

**Caroline Anderson—DELIVERED: ONE FAMILY
Barbara McMahon—TEMPORARY FATHER
Grace Green—TWINS INCLUDED!
Liz Fielding—THE BACHELOR'S BABY**

Available wherever Harlequin books are sold.

HARLEQUIN®
Makes any time special ™

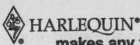

Harlequin truly does make any time special. . . . This year we are celebrating weddings in style!

To help us celebrate, we want you to tell us how wearing the Harlequin wedding gown will make your wedding day special. As the grand prize, Harlequin will offer one lucky bride the chance to **"Walk Down the Aisle"** in the Harlequin wedding gown!

There's more...

For her honeymoon, she and her groom will spend five nights at the **Hyatt Regency Maui.** As part of this five-night honeymoon at the hotel renowned for its romantic attractions, the couple will enjoy a candlelit dinner for two in Swan Court, a sunset sail on the hotel's catamaran, and duet spa treatments.

To enter, please write, in, 250 words or less, how wearing the Harlequin wedding gown will make your wedding day special. The entry will be judged based on its emotionally compelling nature, its originality and creativity, and its sincerity. This contest is open to Canadian and U.S. residents only and to those who are 18 years of age and older. There is no purchase necessary to enter. Void where prohibited. See further contest rules attached. Please send your entry to:

Walk Down the Aisle Contest

In Canada	In U.S.A.
P.O. Box 637	P.O. Box 9076
Fort Erie, Ontario	3010 Walden Ave.
L2A 5X3	Buffalo, NY 14269-9076

You can also enter by visiting www.eHarlequin.com
Win the Harlequin wedding gown and the vacation of a lifetime!
The deadline for entries is October 1, 2001.

PHWDACONT1

HARLEQUIN WALK DOWN THE AISLE TO MAUI CONTEST 1197
OFFICIAL RULES
NO PURCHASE NECESSARY TO ENTER

1. To enter, follow directions published in the offer to which you are responding. Contest begins April 2, 2001, and ends on October 1, 2001. Method of entry may vary. Mailed entries must be postmarked by October 1, 2001, and received by October 8, 2001.

2. Contest entry may be, at times, presented via the Internet, but will be restricted solely to residents of certain georgraphic areas that are disclosed on the Web site. To enter via the Internet, if permissible, access the Harlequin Web site (www.eHarlequin.com) and follow the directions displayed online. Online entries must be received by 11:59 p.m. E.S.T. on October 1, 2001.

   In lieu of submitting an entry online, enter by mail by hand-printing (or typing) on an 8½" x 11" plain piece of paper, your name, address (including zip code), Contest number/name and in 250 words or fewer, why winning a Harlequin wedding dress would make your wedding day special. Mail via first-class mail to: Harlequin Walk Down the Aisle Contest 1197, (in the U.S.) P.O. Box 9076, 3010 Walden Avenue, Buffalo, NY 14269-9076, (in Canada) P.O. Box 637, Fort Erie, Ontario L2A 5X3, Canada.

   Limit one entry per person, household address and e-mail address. Online and/or mailed entries received from persons residing in geographic areas in which Internet entry is not permissible will be disqualified.

3. Contests will be judged by a panel of members of the Harlequin editorial, marketing and public relations staff based on the following criteria:

   - Originality and Creativity—50%
   - Emotionally Compelling—25%
   - Sincerity—25%

   In the event of a tie, duplicate prizes will be awarded. Decisions of the judges are final.

4. All entries become the property of Torstar Corp. and will not be returned. No responsibility is assumed for lost, late, illegible, incomplete, inaccurate, nondelivered or misdirected mail or misdirected e-mail, for technical, hardware or software failures of any kind, lost or unavailable network connections, or failed, incomplete, garbled or delayed computer transmission or any human error which may occur in the receipt or processing of the entries in this Contest.

5. Contest open only to residents of the U.S. (except Puerto Rico) and Canada, who are 18 years of age or older, and is void wherever prohibited by law; all applicable laws and regulations apply. Any litigation within the Province of Quebec respecting the conduct or organization of a publicity contest may be submitted to the Régie des alcools, des courses et des jeux for a ruling. Any litigation respecting the awarding of a prize may be submitted to the Régie des alcools, des courses et des jeux only for the purpose of helping the parties reach a settlement. Employees and immediate family members of Torstar Corp. and D. L. Blair, Inc., their affiliates, subsidiaries and all other agencies, entities and persons connected with the use, marketing or conduct of this Contest are not eligible to enter. Taxes on prizes are the sole responsibility of winners. Acceptance of any prize offered constitutes permission to use winner's name, photograph or other likeness for the purposes of advertising, trade and promotion on behalf of Torstar Corp., its affiliates and subsidiaries without further compensation to the winner, unless prohibited by law.

6. Winners will be determined no later than November 15, 2001, and will be notified by mail. Winners will be required to sign and return an Affidavit of Eligibility form within 15 days after winner notification. Noncompliance within that time period may result in disqualification and an alternative winner may be selected. Winners of trip must execute a Release of Liability prior to ticketing and must possess required travel documents (e.g. passport, photo ID) where applicable. Trip must be completed by November 2002. No substitution of prize permitted by winner. Torstar Corp. and D. L. Blair, Inc., their parents, affiliates, and subsidiaries are not responsible for errors in printing or electronic presentation of Contest, entries and/or game pieces. In the event of printing or other errors which may result in unintended prize values or duplication of prizes, all affected game pieces or entries shall be null and void. If for any reason the Internet portion of the Contest is not capable of running as planned, including infection by computer virus, bugs, tampering, unauthorized intervention, fraud, technical failures, or any other causes beyond the control of Torstar Corp. which corrupt or affect the administration, secrecy, fairness, integrity or proper conduct of the Contest, Torstar Corp. reserves the right, at its sole discretion, to disqualify any individual who tampers with the entry process and to cancel, terminate, modify or suspend the Contest or the Internet portion thereof. In the event of a dispute regarding an online entry, the entry will be deemed submitted by the authorized holder of the e-mail account submitted at the time of entry. Authorized account holder is defined as the natural person who is assigned to an e-mail address by an Internet access provider, online service provider or other organization that is responsible for arranging e-mail address for the domain associated with the submitted e-mail address. **Purchase or acceptance of a product offer does not improve your chances of winning.**

7. Prizes: (1) Grand Prize—A Harlequin wedding dress (approximate retail value: $3,500) and a 5-night/6-day honeymoon trip to Maui, HI, including round-trip air transportation provided by Maui Visitors Bureau from Los Angeles International Airport (winner is responsible for transportation to and from Los Angeles International Airport) and a Harlequin Romance Package, including hotel accomodations (double occupancy) at the Hyatt Regency Maui Resort and Spa, dinner for (2) two at Swan Court, a sunset sail on Kiele V and a spa treatment for the winner (approximate retail value: $4,000); (5) five runner-up prizes of a $1000 gift certificate to selected retail outlets to be determined by Sponsor (retail value $1000 ea.). Prizes consist of only those items listed as part of the prize. Limit one prize per person. All prizes are valued in U.S. currency.

8. For a list of winners (available after December 17, 2001) send a self-addressed, stamped envelope to: Harlequin Walk Down the Aisle Contest 1197 Winners, P.O. Box 4200 Blair, NE 68009-4200 or you may access the www.eHarlequin.com Web site through January 15, 2002.

Contest sponsored by Torstar Corp., P.O. Box 9042, Buffalo, NY 14269-9042, U.S.A.

PHWDACONT2

NEARLYWEDS

Almost at the altar— will these *nearlyweds* become *newlyweds*?

Harlequin Romance® is delighted to invite you to some special weddings! Yet these are no ordinary weddings. Our beautiful brides and gorgeous grooms only *nearly* make it to the altar—before fate intervenes.

But the story doesn't end there.... Find out what happens in these tantalizingly emotional novels!

Authors to look out for include:

Leigh Michaels—The Bridal Swap
Liz Fielding—His Runaway Bride
Janelle Denison—The Wedding Secret
Renee Roszel—Finally a Groom
Caroline Anderson—The Impetuous Bride

Available wherever Harlequin books are sold.

HARLEQUIN®
Makes any time special ™

PARENTS WANTED

Families in the making!

In the orphanage of a small Australian town
called Bay Beach are little children desperately
in need of love, and dreaming of their very
own family....

The answer to their dreams can also be found
in Bay Beach! Couples who are destined for
each other—even if they don't know it yet.
Brought together by love for these tiny
children, can they find true love themselves—
and finally become a real family?

Titles in this series by fan-favorite
MARION LENNOX are

A Child in Need—(April HR #3650)
Their Baby Bargain—(July HR #3662)

Look out for further Parents Wanted stories
in Harlequin Romance®, coming soon!

Available wherever Harlequin Books are sold.

HARLEQUIN®
Makes any time special ®

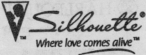